MULGARA

MULGARA

THE NECROMANCER'S WILL

DAVID ROSE

A VIREO BOOK | RARE BIRD BOOKS
LOS ANGELES, CALIF.

This is a Genuine Vireo Book

A Vireo Book | Rare Bird Books
453 South Spring Street, Suite 302
Los Angeles, CA 90013
rarebirdbooks.com

For more information, address:
A Vireo Book | Rare Bird Books Subsidiary Rights Department
453 South Spring Street, Suite 302
Los Angeles, CA 90013

Set in Dante

Printed in the United States

10 9 8 7 6 5 4 3 2 1

Publisher's Cataloging-in-Publication Data

Names: Rose, James David, author.
Title: Mulgara: The Necromancer's Will / David Rose.
Description: First Trade Paperback Original Edition | A Vireo Book |
New York, NY; Los Angeles, CA: Rare Bird Books, 2019.
Identifiers: ISBN 9781947856882
Subjects: LCSH Magic—Fiction. | Wizards—Fiction. | Fantasy. |
BISAC FICTION / Fantasy / Action & Adventure.
Classification: LCC PS3618.O7835 M85 2019 | DDC 813.6—dc23

"A hidden grace in this horrible place, come loping and leaping
with breath. The fugitive flowers in the malefic bowers,
the captors of beauty and death."

—Denom Vandahl, *Poems of the Classics*

Contents

Irion's Tale

A S A YOUNG NECROMANCER, when necromancy was still legal, my great-uncle Maecidion had climbed the ranks of our House to perch on its highest seat. The only man in history to put the Conqueror to negotiation now lay still.

After a funeral where my family thronged together in the ornate blacks of mourning, a gathering of mostly strangers had weathered the height of the rainy season, paraded under the half-finished statues of Do-Gooder's Row, and now sat and squirmed.

I, Irion Ordrid, had to suffer this charade, administered by a barrister calling off names that made me want to kill. My scalp never took to growing hair, making it all the easier to wipe the sweat from my brow in this oppressive heat. What I was witnessing I could hardly bear. I locked my pointed jaw, so as not to speak. Our House was in no shortage of enemies; but unlike the villainous House of Rogaire, too many had actually come to my family's reading and now brushed and breathed against me.

I thanked my eyes for being set deep in my face, for in the gloom they were unable to give away who I razored with passing glances.

Cackles erupted. A crone hobbled her way to the barrister's desk and was bequeathed the jabbering head of a Scepter. Scepters, once elected, answered only to Apex Scepters. The Apexes answered only to the Conqueror—the aforementioned reclusive and ultimate leader of our dismal lands.

This head that I watched, whose jaw agonized moans out from its mummified flesh, belonged to a legislative slug who in life garnered fame for outlawing necromancy in Rehleia. Now he caused great mirth, pleading with us users of the black arts to only return him to death. Our gleeful responses made the dear thing weep dust for tears. While the world gazed upon his tomb, mistaking that he rested in peace, he would be suffering long after even Do-Gooder's Row was one day complete.

My amusement having been temporarily fondled, I was brought back to the day's ugliness when a jar of my great-uncle's Ghorlaxium went to the warlock who sat beside me. Blossoming only one day per year, its purple petals were unparalleled in their ability to hold an apparition in thrall. An assortment of torture devices, books, scrolls, and various other clutter went to smiling new owners.

But the mob soon joined me in my outrage.

✧✧✧

RUMORS THAT MAECIDION ORDRID was dying had caused great unease. When he died, or so went the most common thread of gossip from the bawling, typical, average, flinching Rehleian, demons would erupt from the earth and take my great-uncle "back"—a charitable act as they could ever have hoped for, except that the demons were reportedly going to grab all the innocent souls they could before scampering back to Hell.

Those less inclined to listen to the holy dribble of Chapwyn priests were more worried that our land—only a decade removed from total warfare—would re-splinter. The Metropolitan Ward—dumb faces in even dumber uniforms charged with policing Rehleia and its three cities—they wouldn't be able to hold back *this* chaotic tide. Haggling farmers in the market tossed speculations of inevitable doom as hearty as heads of lettuce and copper coin. An Ordrid civil war was a top contender, how my aunts and cousins would send the world to cinders by pulling in various secular powers.

Perhaps more reasonably feared: if the powers who built roads instead of weaved magic became convinced that my house, the mighty House of Ordrid, had weakened to a critical point. Our annihilation had usually just been furtive Chapwyn church talk, or so I had always been told. But trying to eliminate our entire tribe— the same tribe that once rose legions of skeletons with the wiggle of an onyx-ringed finger—the people feared it would merely provoke us into summoning more unearthly allies.

No, a good sheep of the new land would prefer if incorrigibles would just die in jail, or maybe unclog their plumbing, and then vanish until needed again. Though I was from a lower branch, it boiled me that some referred to my kinsmen with the blissful condescension of one who's never had a knife to their neck. But it gave me some reprieve too, knowing their wishful thinking was different than actually taking up arms against us, the most notorious lot in all Rehleia.

Before attending the clandestine school we dead-raisers call the lyceum, as all men from prominent families must, I'd suffered the maps and history lessons of a primary education. But unlike the Ouvarnias perched in the flamboyant city of Pelliul, or the politician-churning House of Lotgard, I find such learning only useful now to pinpoint my own family's prominence.

Rehleia is a knotted peninsula, like an afflicted fist stuck out on a withered arm. Pushing east and connecting Rehleia to the Other Lands is our Red Isthmus—named so for the rivers of blood that had once flown from its narrow hinterland down into the sea.

At this east our lands meet the world of Azad, a desert kingdom littered with pit fires and bulb-topped minarets built low to the sand.

Above Azad: Serabandantilith, raped by Azad and Rehleia once they figured out that ceasing their own war allowed for the pillaging of their weaker neighbor. Azad took the land. Rehleia took the people and the gold. The former mixing with the dark Suelans, beefing up Rehleia's much-celebrated slave class.

A few years after the Rehleian Years of Peace had officially commenced, trade began over the Red Isthmus, sweeping aside all its broken swords and lances.

And as far as Rehleia is concerned, the House of Ordrid's stronghold is here in Nilghorde. On a city hill above the brick wilderness, our family keep looks over the western sea. In this jagged crown, stowed in some charnel nook, the great Maecidion had finally died.

It was long argued over: when he, rightfully the most infamous of the province's celebrities, actually discorporated. His form was kept together, I was told, but despite diplomatic transactions with the demonic, means of animation still slowly seeped from the flesh as it rose from bone.

Most of the estate was already in the possession of Maecidion's most esoteric clutch: sisters Ophelia and Lialifer, cousins to my mother, and Morfil Ordrid, whose entire life had been dutifully in the shadow of his Lord and pedagogue. But that didn't stop the vile throng from attending today. All were in accord; given just a goblet by his wishes held the highest prestige in this society others dare called foul.

The air was a kennel's warmth, sinking down us and settling on the floor. The room itself was but stone and shadow, both made known only by a ring of dull candlelight. In this ring's center, attendants pulled chairs out from under the other, bites were delivered and tended to, and murmurs slithered amongst the bequeathings yet-to-be.

The barrister—looking as if batting away thoughts of being skewered—readied himself and continued reading the last will and testament of Maecidion the Virulent.

WHEN MAECIDION'S FAMILIAR WAS read off to anyone other than an Ordrid, the only thing that brought me to a fuller froth was that it went to Denoreyph Belot. Belot!—a self-important narcissist who cared about such frivolities as charm spells. For pursuing a discipline outside necromancy, he was especially hated. His dimmer critics obsessed over this feat, and obsessed all the dimmer that those who didn't join them in their disgust had been in fact charmed themselves. I joined them, that and then some. Arrogant, Belot's silk swayed as he strutted up and seized the imp in its cage.

Belot! That prancing girl, I thought, reeling back to spit. *Imp belongs in the family.* I watched him until he sat back down to preen his sash and cross his legs like an actor.

Bickering soon gave way to the normalcy of hissing. More of Maecidion's chambers were cleared out and soon snatched by their corresponding names.

I hadn't received so much as a wall sconce. *One more carbuncled witch from the hills being called up to lust over my family's possessions and a stink bomb may have to be the first in an arsenal of unhinged aggressions.* Yes, a lover of caustic tricks am I. My pockets can range from such simplicities as a spool of yarn or a malodorous vial to more severe components that help build spells able to make one wish to see their own mother couple with mountain trolls. A quick inventory proved I'd brought a few rather useful—

The den was pure noise. It was as if that Scepter's headless body had pushed up the doors of his tomb, stumbled through the streets, and then led a pod of the Metropolitan Ward to hack up us patrons. The uproar became awe, then it became envy. A statue had been placed on the barrister's desk.

Seen in the clasped hands of every portrait of Maecidion to ever cover a sullen wall, the statue, a hand itself, was made of pure lapis lazuli. The size of your average man's, strains of gold feathered and swirled in the deep blue of its outstretched fingers. In its palm, three faces made a row. The outer two left trails at its base near the wrist, thus completing a long-agreed-upon murmur that they resembled haunted tadpoles. And these both seemed poised to circle the central visage; caught in an eternal, devilish sneer.

Astonished grumbles carried "Morfil" and "…for who then?" Chair legs squeaked. Hopefuls rushed the desk. A fistfight erupted.

I didn't need to tear down the aisle or crawl over any cursed heads. I knew it well. This peculiar ornament had been in Maecidion's possession long before a single Suelan slave had been brought to Rehleian shores. It had also been previously owned by other powerful Ordrid leaders, long returned to oblivion.

What would it would mean if the Virulent left it to me? What misery would be deserving to anyone other than I, if I were not to receive her?

And while I'd been lost in such thoughts, fiddling in my pockets, a name had been read.

When it was announced for a second time, the gathering boiled over from gasped vacuum to pure hysteria. Slugging his way forward, Gormorster Toadly, as surprised as his howling detractors, knew now the first announcement hadn't been a trick of his ears. With a rodent's face sitting on top of several glistening chins, the gormandizer smelling of sweat, sweets, and necrophilia looked to be the unlikeliest of all attendants to receive an invitation, let alone this choice artifact.

I was soon leading the mob, hurling insults and looking for an available chair not bolted to the floor. While an imp was highly sought after, this was an heirloom. It going to anyone outside the House was detestable, and all the more foul to the senses that a flatulent glutton-wretch like Toadly would now own it. I had to wrestle down a misfit trying to rise from deep within me. Reappraising the genius of my recently deceased patriarch was by all accounts an ill strategy, even if he was dead.

Toadly gloated and giggled, showboating by a series of squinty-eyed sneers. He held the statue like a pageant winner or a proud new father.

I burst open the doors and marched out into the lobby. *Last wishes be damned.* That inner-misfit was winning, and it was straight to the coat closest. I pilfered through the dampened garb. It didn't take long. I found the raven-feathered collar.

"Belot," I heard myself say, "Still wearing lyceum monstrosities." I opened the coal coat and rifled through it. A smile broke free across my face by the second or third pocket. Charm spells were one thing, but Belot loved a single practice above all else; raping the minds of the dying. It took the meeting of two special powders to enact such a spell—two powders I then replaced with two components you'd never wish to see conjoined.

When the crowd hobbled out from the hall, I melted back into the swarm. Some were angry, most disappointed, but those were more their ways than any. A few of the more brazen cursed Maecidion before catching themselves mid-utterance to look over their shoulder, staring into my disapproving glare. Before long the hall and the coat closet were all but empty. The fiends returned to their lairs to, as Chapwyn priests so ardently report, brew their irksome things; slither under the moonlight; and invoke, summon, and fondle the dead.

❀❀❀

FROM THE LOWER BRANCH indeed, I would one day be feared and exalted for this warpath that I'd undertook. I kicked the door open and pulled the clerk in by her hair. In a dark corner serving only as a residence for spiders and scrolls, I uncupped my hand from her mouth and put one finger to my lips.

The Nilghorde Hall of Records was monstrous. The main doors towered green with midsections of stained glass, but deep in its catacombs the door swinging shut behind me peeled three layers of different paint. The central corridor had been a murmuring hive of footsteps. Moving about, this way and that, irate merchants and disputing tenants slammed doors and stamped down stairs.

Now only flickers of their shadows made way to me. I was at the Residency Office; used only by the Ward and magistrate's apprentices, and maybe that was why it was at the end of such a long tunnel. To my good fortune, only one clerk toiled in lamplight behind the reception desk. To my bad fortune, I'd spent the last of my Ghorlaxium on the potion I'd made for her.

When boiled in small doses and cut with Leaves of Luka, Ghorlaxium makes the living spew out all they know. I knelt above the clerk in dual dismay. I needed another batch; if all went well, this woman who'd gulped the potion past the edge of my blade would lead me forward. But, more pressing, an overdose didn't kill—*that* would at least give me some options. If only I had the time. But rather than death, my miscalculation had resulted in a rolling blabber.

"Kornard kept on," she said, looking past me with bulging eyes. "My sister couldn't pla…please him after having her baby. The baby that woulda been *ours* coulda never have been." I considered killing her. "Mother woulda never…" She trailed off into a string of inaudibles. I gazed around. Somewhere in this mess of boxes, scrolls, drawers, wobbling towers of books there was a name, and with it an address. "Mother woulda killed all four of us!"

After an eternity, the abortion confession ceased.

"Are you scared?"

"Terrified" the clerk said, her voice as flat as her hair matting the floorboards. She lay like an open-casket funeral, even when I took my hands off her wrists.

"Are barristers designated by duty?" Her mouth opened but said nothing. "Here, in this office?" I added.

"Why…yes, by specialty you could say."

"Good," I said, petting her head. Then, spacing my words out to eliminate any more blunders, "Where can I find magistrates in charge of probate? In charge of wills?"

"I don't know."

I pressed down on her wrists. "Then *who* does?"

"Yodïor, my boss."

"And he comes?"

"Soon."

I'd heard of a trick back at the lyceum for keeping them quiet. "Make a noise now only if you've never lied."

It worked.

✢ ✢ ✢

NOT A ONE, NOT a larval lawyer or single member of the Ward, approached the reception desk. Having deprived the clerk of her apron, I sat behind the slab and watched the lamp oil burn. The central corridor's shadows weakened, fading down from what was once a stamping march to a few furtive slinks and far calls. The lamp smoke grew thicker, my back began to ache, and then a silhouette grew as it approached. A black dot soon emerged in lamplight, turning into a lumpy man whose glasses reflected shifts of yellow and orange.

"You must be my supervisor," I said, putting down the sheet of parchment I'd been pretending to read. "Yoddy, Yodi."

"Who—where is Loona?"

"That was her name, Loona. She went home, sick." The little man's face glistened with sweat he'd worked up while walking down the hall. But that wasn't the only reason he was sweating. Looks over his shoulder and nervous scratches to his crotch and ass told me everything. "I'm a temp."

"A temp? We don't—"

His attempt to flee was as muffled as his screams. The sheet of parchment balled and shoved in his mouth, my blade separating his

17

chins, Yodïor kicked as I lifted his feet off the stones. The little door with the awful paint swung open for a second time.

"No!" Yodïor screamed before I kicked him in the gut. Gasping to regain his breath, he lay in Loona's blood, which by way of an unfortunate slip, I too felt: cooled and congealing. I'd slit her throat when the potion had worn off. A means to an end no driven man has time to worry over. Though she was on her stomach and this Yodïor lay on his back, I mused for but a moment how they lay locked in a stare, unifying two on opposing sides of the grave.

"As you wish to live," I crawled on top of him, "cease your whimpering and answer me." He nodded, emitting squeaks that sounded like a girl's. "Where can I find magistrates in charge of probate? In charge of wills?"

✤✤✤

GIVEN THE ROOM'S VASTNESS and the excrement indicating hidden routes from the sewers, they'd be gnawed bones by the time anyone found them. But my thoughts were elsewhere. The will reading was only a day old; I clutched the top half of a municipal parchment. The top was all I needed. The choices were an insult, almost arbitrary, as if the barrister had written the will the day of, just to see the crowd's reaction.

I found the barrister. In his bedchambers the lawman frantically swore that he'd merely read the will as it had been written, a conviction that remained unwavering up to the last dagger slash.

✤✤✤

WE ORDRIDS ARE ALL fond of the moon. I gazed upon it, the great beacon of my House. I thought I'd heard it call my name as I stumbled through all the graves. Blossoming on the vines that grew on elder headstones, Orphedilias opened to vector in its gentle light. Poets and ninnies like Belot would have stopped to ogle at their shape perhaps.

I came to the graveyard's center, the Maedraderium. I halted and stood before the new obelisk. Black and gold, jutting out of a cluster of pediment tombs, this robust monument to my great-uncle now towered. His Virulence had worked in startling mystery at times, not issuing an immediate and savage revenge on the House of Rogaire was chief among my confusions.

But now this. Of all the places to be buried.

The common man was at best a two-legged dog, and Maecidion had willed his obelisk in a graveyard hardly good enough for such a dog's dead fleas. What unfathomable nonsense! He could have been exalted a mile high; future generations of Ordrids and wide-eyed gawkers would have been straining their necks. The prattling on about the Maedraderium being City Cemetery's wealthy centerpiece meant little to me. Most still just called this island of stones, more a small city of venerated dead, "Laugher's Lot." If it had any meaning at all, I'd have to guess it derived from the morticians, mirthfully swelling the lot as their coffers filled.

I held in my hand a bottle of that corn liquor, Spiritual Oppressor. I took another pull. "I am sorry, dearest Lord," I said, "but I cannot see to it. See to it that I leave your wishes untouched." And why shouldn't I feel this way? The very man whose will I was rebelling against had once made such bold moves in his own time. Would he—could he—at least appreciate my ambitions, providing the impetus to be so bold? The reading now three days old, it troubled me no less.

Swaying, emptied bottle in hand, I arched my back and stuck out my chest. Behind Maecidion's obelisk, the moon, a vast orb hinting at tainted cheese, greeted me like a brother.

I hadn't come to talk to an obelisk; just a thoughtful gesture along the way. I tossed the Spiritual Oppressor and continued to a hamlet on the edge of the graves.

✤✤✤

I CROUCHED IN THE hedges like some sneak thief. But such humiliations were necessary. Toadly's tower wasn't so much a tower, more a farmer's silo, complete with thatched rotting top, giving the whole thing the appearance of a giant's refracting phallus that had caught Thina's Poxy. It loomed so close to City Cemetery that I couldn't tell if the neglected hedge, grown wild with weeds and brambers, belonged to Toadly or to Nilghorde.

I'd sobered quick enough, perhaps expedited by having suffered bouts of rain.

Shadows conjoined and shifted behind Toadly's windows. Within, long bouts of silence would rip open in an instant with bellows of ignoramus mirth. Of all the nights for such a home to play host to the living. But as I adjusted a troublesome root for the third time, Toadly's door swung open and out poured the filth. Though the departing gaggle was of several classes, they struck me as acquainted scoundrels, tarrying under a lone lamplight before finally leaving.

I froze. A pack of other men scrambled out from concealing hedges across from my own. The moment I began to rise I'd been put back down, reduced to peering out through leaves. The pack moved from one shadow to the next, then broke down Toadly's door.

Toadly had enemies like snakes have scales: I among them. It would have been amusing if a brood of brothers with their stone-cutting father at the helm had burst in to avenge the lamentable state of one of the many concubines that had made Toadly famous. But the pack's look of intent villainy disallowed such fantasies. The thumps and sounds of breaking glass and feet pounding up and down stairwells were at the bidding of, I knew beyond a doubt, some other fiend who'd also attended the will reading.

"If it is gone—" the rest I hissed into my hand. A sudden headache needled my skull: Someone had beat me to it. I'd sat around, pitying myself with a liquor bottle, and it may have just cost me everything. I felt a shame that my conscious would not fully allow. An image of brewing tricks and potions on the lowest branch in all Necrodom faded, and the part of my mind where words were found refit itself. *The puma who slept through the deer migrating while dreaming of idle sheep.* I gripped my dagger's handle. Rain pooled on leaves and ran down my neck.

After some while, the thugs reentered the street, and with their reappearance the vice-clamp around my head loosened its grip. On the ground, behind one of the larger men, was a mammoth bag, sowed tight and soaked with blood. I'd never quite experienced disappointment and elation at once, until just then.

One of the oldest Ordrids ever to be penned to a scroll, Prince Basofial had enjoyed a parade of carnage, yet was denied the blood dipping of his own morning star. Seeing Toadly dead and stuffed into a sack, I couldn't help but wonder if this is how the long-dead prince had felt when the droves of poor had killed the aristocracy over in Quinnari?

I was again frozen. The grunting shadows were dragging Toadly right toward me.

Grunts became words. Soon, shadows became scowls and leather gloves. Leading them, an over-muscled lug stowed a petite arm that had been severed at the elbow into his belt. All it would take is one alley-grade wizard among them to route me out, one of the lugs then pulling me up by my neck like a chicken. My crouching intensified to a curl, my dagger blade tight against my palm. If I were one of the Ordrids who prayed, I would have done so as legs burst open the hedge.

The trail of boot prints and a sweep like a crocodile's slide met the grass of City Cemetery. "Even split" and "not this rutterkin, ya pansy nob" became grunts once more, and soon, save for pats of rain, there was silence.

"It's been invaded by a pack of gorillas," I spit, having entered Toadly's trash heap. Knowing him, this parlor had always probably been a clogged artery of trinkets and spoiled meat. But whatever stage of slow explosion it had once been, it had burst like a zit. All was everywhere. Everything but the army of candles; hung about on sconces, stuck into cracks, and resting on frames of draperies that had somehow been spared.

The last I had seen of the invaders, they were making their way toward the other side of the cemetery. In front of me now were the remnants of their night's work: furniture upended, books torn to pieces, rather insignificant parts of the home mangled beyond repair. I would never be sure what a fire prodder, broken in three, could have ever hoped to contain.

Still, this mangling may have only meant that they never found what they were looking for.

I rushed up the first stairway. Near the top it was the swaying legs that I saw first, and behind them a large and well-lit room.

Without the command of their master, the female slaves exhibited all the fuller their state of unlife. Dull, lidless eyes, nestled in sallow faces, alive but not alive, dead but not dead, stared at me as I summited the stairs.

Passing between them was like walking through a forest where all the seeds had been planted in exact, nauseating little rows. Behind the last row of slaves was a giant bed. It was covered in blood; reflecting the halo of candles that hung above. That he'd been killed right before one of his wretched orgies delighted me. From a new angle, I now saw that concubines closer to the bed had been sprayed by his blood. Their resemblance to a military formation suggested this was their position of maintenance when not bringing up a pot of cooked sea slugs or performing their sexual duties. Toadly's reputation for incessantly leering at the female backside was all the more confirmed, as the swaying columns faced away from where he'd slept and self-fondled.

Not a cauldron was left unturned. I shimmied up chimney shafts, settling for stretching a crawling arm up the ones that I couldn't inspect further. I ended up mimicking the prior stampede up and down the stairs in a fever. I turned the place end over end—thrice over what the goons had done—but Maecidion's lapis lazuli hand was gone.

After I'd found a surviving vase to shatter to dust, my fury cooled. I gave the undead slut who'd had most her arm hacked off a prompt smack on her ass. The leathery cheek gave in all the way to the bone. I was soon staring up at the candles. Their shafts were hardly shorter than when I'd entered the tower. It hadn't been long.

Toadly's killers had been thorough in their search but careless in their escape. I followed their boot prints and spilled keepsakes all the way through the heart of City Cemetery. I was led right between Maecidion's obelisk and the bottle I'd tossed. Picking up the trinkets and smearing the mud and blood of heavy boot prints would keep the Ward out of this—in the rare chance an investigation into someone like Toadly's disappearance caught the fancy of an aspiring shift-lead. That concern, however weak or strong, evaporated when I saw where the boot tracks had ended.

❦❦❦

"THEEE REEEVENGE I SHALL enact upon you," Toadly moaned inside Belot's parlor. His curses didn't come so much from his mouth, but gurgled from the slash that ran across his throat. Blood and lung-froth spilled over and ran down to the table he was bound to.

I stood outside Belot's window, moon and graves to my back. It was a matter of convenience that Gormorster Toadly and Denoreyph Belot chose to live on opposing sides of City Cemetery. For those of us privy to such skirmishes, it created a sort of chess board between the two, rumored to have been encouraged by a committee of Scepters to maintain low property value in the surrounding areas. The demands of the dead had leveled entire city blocks to make way for new rows of headstones and cheap tombs. Yet these domiciles of the two corpse-diddlers remained: paragons of tradition.

I scanned the room. A place for poor work, surely; Belot stood at the foot of the table. Behind Belot, tall as a man, were shelves heavied by standard potions and jars. On the other side of this table, Belot faced the material he used when playing necromancer. The stack of corpses appeared untampered, having died at ages from elder to infant, and now lay like firewood in different stages of decomposition. And above everything, attached to a ceiling hook, watching from an iron birdcage, sat my imp. Seemingly content to forever study the shelves; feet, arms, and nose poking out from the caging, the imp, I rejoiced, must have refused to imprint with Belot. Imprisoned until it assimilated to its new master, the little fiend was reduced to sit and watch.

Strapped down at his wrists and his ankles, purple with fresh death, Toadly could only squirm and weep. "Youuuu," slid off Toadly's swollen tongue as his eyes rolled upward against his will.

"Oh, silence now," Belot said, hands on his hips. "If you absolutely refuse to tell me where it is, I can't let you rest. You're doing this to yourself, you know."

Delight and intrigue fought for a superior position within me. It was a delight to witness Toadly be tortured, and even more a delight to savor these moments right before Belot's big surprise. I knew what he was up to, for Belot, if anything, was consistent. Though Toadly's flesh was now dead, his mind again lived, one Belot had brought back, and now began to dominate.

Where it is? It struck me like a lightning bolt. Abducting Toadly and executing this reanimation had to be for a good reason. *It*—Belot could only be referring to the hand statue! If Belot didn't already have it, then where did Toadly have it hidden? I glared through the window as I redeveloped my plan. I could usurp minds too.

Belot's arms began to rise and Toadly howled in accordance. My luck had turned, for I couldn't have asked for more perfect timing.

Baying in protest, Toadly was feeling every thought he'd ever held suck toward his captor like warmed honey dripping from a wooden spoon. Belot, fueled by the frantic kicks and pleas for mercy through a slit throat, inched closer to putting Toadly in the state all necromancers feared most. For while what body one could occupy could change form, and the very boundaries of life and death could be hopped over like a naughty child hopping over a line deemed off-limits, the mind itself was the sole source of a being, to be preserved and unmolested at all cost. Belot's arms raised, he held the separate powders for this spell in each hand. Upon their union, Toadly would divulge all, and go forever to his grave defiled.

If I hadn't switched out the powders the day of the reading.

When Belot's hands met, he lit up as if made of lamp oil. A detonation erupted. Belot became ghastly whistles in a burgeoning gown of flames. Toadly, eyes wide and elated, showed even the undead savored comeuppance.

I kicked open the door. Toadly flopped his head toward the noise of my boot, just as soon recognizing me and returning to his panic. "That blue hand," I said, looming over the gluttonous wretch, "is in as many paintings in my home as pulseless whores are in yours. And you thought you'd have it?!" The pleasure of knowing I'd suck up every drop of Toadly's miserable mind was second only to the joy of hearing Belot's screams.

Perhaps I owed my late great-uncle an immediate and roaring "thank you". When Belot was bequeathed what he had been, it was the final spur in my side to do the world a favor and rid it of him. That I would now own the imp, Toadly's mind for an hour, and, with the latter executed correctly, the family heirloom too: I breathed in the smoke as fires died on the charred meat at my boot toe.

How the zest for a meal is conquered by the desire to couple with a woman for the first time, and how retreating from a crumbling building would triumph over said coupling, my attention had been torn from Toadly to the burning of Belot. Now lamentably over, I was able to refocus.

Toadly lay motionless.

I shook his corpse as if trying to rouse a lazy wife from her bed. A sudden nervousness grew inside me, for this wasn't supposed to happen. The preparatory segment of the incantation had been broken, yes, but experience and experimentation suggested that reanimation waned at a much slower rate. Toadly was now fully dead, the normal dead, and secondary and tertiary reanimations were exponentially more difficult.

A sudden adjustment from the imp caused me to glance in the direction of not only its cage, but the bodies below it. Had that window above the corpse-stack always been ajar?

How much time had actually elapsed since Belot had been a crawling bonfire? But this wasn't the only pressing question. Toadly, though a low carcass in comparison to other practitioners that speckled our forbidden world, was not without his craft. There were tricks, hexes, and bedevilments accredited to his name. I was reduced to scratching my head and staring back at my imp.

✳ ✳ ✳

AFTER KICKING TOADLY ONE last time, I sat down and gave it all a laugh. It was all I could do. "Irion Ordrid the Poor Planner" may one day be chiseled into my own obelisk, but I would at least enjoy this next improvisation. Belot would live again.

A few powders from his cabinet later, I'd poured the appropriate line between me and him. The invocations started, Belot's smoldering heap began to twitch.

The waiting was gruesome—not the visuals, but the agony of waiting for reanimation to fulfill. All people, bodies, and species were different, and in time-sensitive moments such as this, all I could do was pace about and kick random corpses. It was when I looked up at my new imp once more that from Belot there burst the grimmest consecution of cries. No less the sounds of the shores of Hell, in this discord was concentrated a hatred in life ripened one thousand fold through death, and by treacherous events of the trip to and back from those shores.

"What causes thee wakening of the Great Denoreyph Belot?" the grizzly skeleton wailed, rising to meatless feet.

"You were always so lousy with components," I said. Belot's skull cocked back in a sign of recognition. "Laying them about the room, labeling them in that thick gaudy ink, like a man going blind."

"For thissss, you summon me? To reminisce about dead lyceum days, and the women who juiced my bed next to your celibate cot?"

The skeleton, draped only in charred flesh, stepped closer, ribs stuck out and balled, bony fists cast back. In Belot's eyeless sockets, I saw the immaterial glimmer.

"Where is the blue hand?"

"That's no concern to me now," Belot hissed. "Let us ask our dear friend—Oh, Gormorster. Oh, look—he's dead, deader than I."

"If he still has it, I'll get it from him. We both know it," I said. "Professor Fryte did it with that stitched-up fuck she had locked up in her closet. We both were there. You remember. You may be," my smirk broadened, "excuse me, *used* to be an overrate, labeling your childish jars and cheating on tests, but you know how usurpation works."

Belot blew out a laugh that paralleled his recent cry back to life in both its volume and hysteria. "That may be. But I always remembered to close my windows." Everything in the parlor that could move stared at a lone open window. "My old freights looking a wee light there, Irion."

"What are you saying?"

Belot erupted in cackles. "Toadly is goooone, Irion." No, Toadly was laying on the table. Yet as I listened to Belot hiss, practices that I'd heard of but had never seen myself began to encroach my mind. Casting one's essence into another form was a feat Toadly had been persecuted over and heralded for. It would have taken time to weave, but in my savoring of the fire, I had given him such a vital commodity. I looked once more at the stack of corpses below the open window. "Ah, yes, yesss. Good, Irion. Toadly is now," I heard Belot saying. There *had* been a body there, one that was there no longer. It had been—Belot's words then seeped into my ear, finishing my dreadful thought: "a babe."

"You're going to help me find him!" I shouted. "Fire has seemed to have forgotten you the craft, Belot! This," I flapped my hand at his hilarious state, "this is just the beginning. This living mind of yours, being used to mock and riddle as wasteful as done in life, it just came from me. Me!" I took a hard step forward. "We both know I can just as easily extract from it, as you were about to do to that fat lump of shit over there."

As best a skull with sporadic rigging can, Belot quivered. I opened my coat and withdrew a vial. Belot's bony hands made for my neck as I opened up the vial and drank down its contents. The bitter syrup was exactly what Belot had drunk to own the mind of Toadly. I felt my will wrap around Belot's like a chain. The effect would not last forever, but maybe long enough.

Whether to pose a less startling silhouette, or maybe the damage of flame had made open night air feel like dancing razors, or maybe the vanity of Belot in life somehow held in his state of chattel-undead—for whatever reason, he draped himself in one of his black silken cloaks and followed his master out the door.

At the base of the open window I discovered a baby's footprints. They had scampered into the wet lawn of City Cemetery.

###

WE'D STALKED CLEAR ACROSS City Cemetery. The footprints cut through those of Belot's thugs, darted for Toadly's tower straight through the Maedraderium, but then surprised me by veering a sharp left. It led us through an embankment of streets and buildings that met a corner of the graveyard. We now lurked inside a large nursery, having found the final footprint at its lanterned door. Toadly, the clever little rat.

Toadly, the clever little rat, Belot ideated, reconfirming that I now owned his mind.

Absorbing ourselves into the darkest corners of a nursery bay was easy enough. In the moonlit middle, a row of cribs cooed stirs and kicked up blankets. The moon came through the bay's elongated windows, stretching shadows of the cribs long against a back wall.

Start at the far end, I thought at Belot.

Start at the far end, Belot ideated.

Belot moved off, drifting through the moonbeams and then out of my sight. I commenced searching the nearer cribs with a drawn dagger. Toadly needed to be "alive," but I'd certainly sever a fat little leg. Possessed bodies are impelled by stamina and dexterity far greater than the living. I knew it, as did Toadly.

I peered into cradle after cradle, looking to see if the miserable trickster had occupied an empty one. After scanning the spaces underneath, I stood to keep an eye on Belot, slowly sailing through the rows and columns.

What is that? Belot and I thought at the same time. Lamplight approached, flat-footed plods coming right behind it. A narrow passageway that until then had remained hidden now bore an attendant.

I had Belot coil under his nearest crib. Then I pressed my back against my nearest wall.

A nursemaid, lamp cast out in front of her houndish nose, hobbled in.

Legs. Walking. Words I felt Belot think freely, almost whispering right over his teeth. From my obscure angle, it appeared the woman was passing the crib he hid under. *I'm on the ground*, Belot thought, making my heart leap, for my dominion over him was already beginning to wane. Making matters more perilous, he must have said it aloud. The woman had stopped. The lantern shook.

If Belot was discovered under a crib like some hideous snake, the woman's shrieks would startle every babe and armed guard within a mile. Dagger honed, using each passing crib to conceal me, I made my way to them.

"Smoked pork?" the woman said. A lone crib now from her back, I saw her shrug her shoulders then resume her rounds. I sheathed my dagger.

We continued searching, and we may have done so all night if it weren't for the imp flashing me a sudden vision. Yes, the imp. I at first elated, for this meant it knew it belonged to the House of Ordrid. The greatest of familiars, when one is joined with such a little fiend, the imp allows its master its cunning, to hear through its ears, and, I now gaped, the horrid sights seen through its eyes.

It showed me an entire scene unfold all in one instant:

Toadly was climbing through the open window back at Belot's. His new hands he must have loathed, but they grasped the window superbly, as did his new legs, having bursting up from the ground below. His laughter while in his obese true form had sounded to me once like a creature being boiled alive. But now, as a bluish infant mottled in decay, they were little giggles. I had been tricked! He must have double backed as I made a fool of myself in the damn nursery. The giggles made their way into

Belot's parlor as Toadly scaled down the stool and apron and jumped nimbly to the floor.

It gave me some reprieve to see that Toadly stood over his old body, lying there dead and humiliated. I am sure in some singular way he thanked me too. For I had given to Belot a fate that any captive would dream to see their captor suffer. But more than that, cringing at the thought of the amount of his laughter that had been aimed at me, by killing Belot I had freed Toadly's mind...and had even given him time to escape.

Toadly walked around his body, his current head no higher than the plateau of the rack that held his former self.

Toadly stopped and picked up a chunk of blackened flesh. He then dropped it and sprang from the floor like a cricket, landing on his own bloated corpse.

Toadly was going to try to not only reanimate his old body, but reassume it! If so, and if he were able to seal himself off and repair his manglings to a semblance of function, Toadly half-alive and enraged could be worse than ten normal men.

Small arms were cast skyward. His baby mouth began to open. What would have been Toadly's booming moan was something quite different. The rites, though uttered perfectly, filled the room with that of a sprite's. The baby's head whipped down. Dollish eyes gazed. Then he cast his head back. Its eyes glossed over with the purest white.

The imp flashed me this—its vision, sending me scrambling back toward Belot's.

⌗⌗⌗

BELOT RAN BEHIND ME as if I were pulling him with a leash. The coming of morning bled into the black surrounding the moon.

That cauldron of shit couldn't have, I thought.

That cauldron couldn't, Belot ideated.

31

My control over Belot was weakening. With a surge, I willed him to stand guard at his open window, while I sweated against his door and caught my breath.

My worry was then confirmed. When I reentered the parlor, I pressed my back against the door, hung my head, and sighed.

The dismal worktable at the center of this dismal room was bare. Near my feet lay the baby, now limp and contorted, as if thrown.

Walking to the table, I stopped at the cage hanging above. The night was far from a loss. I had the imp, one who had already done for me what it only did for those it deemed worthy. Plus, I'd killed the Great—ornate—Denoreyph Belot, and even fulfilled an adolescent fantasy of commanding his corpse around. Toadly would be addressed later, once reorganized and a better plan made.

It was right then that I saw the imp's face change.

###

WHEN I CAME TO, blasting pain flowed from a gash somewhere on the back of my head. I was face down, on the floor, in a pool of my own blood. Belot stood above me. Disenthralled from my dominion, wielding one of his ornamental canes that had surely felled me, meat and teeth sneered and his sockets flashed.

Belot widened his stance. Regripping his weapon, "Not the fate for you I desired," he wailed, "but I haven't the time!" He rose his cane to, I'm sure, beat me to death in as many strikes as he could before oblivion claimed us both. But before the first one fell, Toadly came barreling out of nowhere. In Toadly's hands was a colossal iron spoon from one of Belot's cauldrons.

Though I had managed to roll over, I was still unable yet to rise. Separated only by me lying at their feet, the two then clashed like pit fighters.

When I rolled onto my side, my head exploded in such pain I'd thought for a moment that the damned spoon had found me instead. I watched the melee as an emerged worm watching a street performance. The skeleton was dodging the slow, skull-crushing swoops while hissing his curses. The fat man, almost a light green, gargled through the slice under his bottom-most chin, while his engorged stomach jostled with his violent wiggling. With a loping swing of the giant spoon, something fell out from between two of Toadly's glistening roles.

Landing upright, as if placed by a servant, the lapis lazuli hand stood before me. Toadly's feet and Belot's bones danced as I clasped onto it.

I had it! It was done! Soon Belot would fade, and if I were lucky, while I waited on the floor unnoticed, maybe he'd use that cane to break Toadly's fat head.

From the floor, curiosity and confusion penetrated my euphoria, for right then the imp opened its cage.

My eyes were pulled from the fight when it reached out and stuck its scorpion-stinger fingernail into the lock that had been—or so I'd thought—preventing its flight.

Flew it did, to a shelf to latch its hands around a small black jar. Little bat wings gliding, the imp flew over Belot, Toadly, and myself, and dusted us with its contents.

The blue hand began to thrum. It began to burn my fingers, but I only held it tighter. A moment later I had been pulled to my feet, but by what I could not say. I was standing between both of my enemies. Belot's bones flew against me, sticking to my arms and chest as if attached by paste. Belot's teeth chattered in my ear while Toadly's head was slung back and a fountain of noise and bile erupted from the gash.

It was as if the three of us were standing still while the room spun at a terrible speed. Toadly was smaller now—his eyes glaring up at me while his arms hugged my leg. What looked like maggots squirmed where Belot's large bones had been just a moment before.

"No!" I cried as I heard Belot cry the same. "Not this! Not him!" we cried.

Toadly, now a hideous tadpole, made a slow, close orbit as I felt the putrid itch of Toadly's fusion. Covered in the powder that started this, there was a sudden crowding in my mind.

There was the collection of memory and thoughts that I identified as *Irion*. But there were others too. There was one: a maker of undead slaves and master of his craft. There was another: cruel, cunning, ever-working. Yet there seemed to be a looming fourth being, one who settled on us like a fog. Darker, this insidious force felt much older, and it was this one who I cried out to inexplicably in a dialect from times long ago, "What is thou which touches me?!"

I, Maecidion, then felt a rebirth that few creatures can know. Without eyes I saw; without body I began to feel. "Worry not, young one," I said.

Pathetic whimpers and yelps in the periphery were all that was left of Gormorster Toadly and Denoreyph Belot. "I, I am sorry," that which was still Irion said. "Forgive me, my Lord. There was no way of knowing. I thought maybe, maybe that you had gone mad in your final moments."

Irion was sophomoric, but audacious and physically able. It was why he had been chosen, as both the other two had been chosen for their greatest endowments. Their poor qualities melting away, the synthesis was congealing as that which was still Irion pled, "Your Virulence, please—"

What was once Irion remained only a moment more, a fluttering of two memories: perusing a scroll under candlelight at the lyceum, and then the midnight garden in our family keep, playing with his cousins under the moon. As excited cries carried on the night wind, he ran from his hiding place. Finding his playmates, what was once Irion faded as if never existing at all.

I looked at my hands, then my feet. I breathed in the air of the splendid early morning, then extended my arm for my imp to perch.

⁂

THE MORNING WAS THE shade of gray that always brought rain. *I*, once again, stood at the giant obelisk of Maecidion the Virulent. I was mostly still garbed in Irion's black, adding only one of Belot's black cloaks. A satchel was slung over my shoulder; in it, a few coins and choice components to retackle the world, my beautiful coiled imp, and my lapis lazuli hand.

I smiled at the obelisk. *My* obelisk. The world could see this testament to my departure. The more, the better. Times were changing; that part of *him* had been right. Even an ancient must adapt. The man the world had known as Maecidion was just an earlier vessel, and the predecessor before Maecidion the same. I could hardly contain my amusement; simply clearing out the clutter of a closet was enough to mask my plan. I cared nothing for the recipients at what I'm sure was a riotous hearing, and prior to had laughed as I'd laid dying and Morfil penned their insignificant names.

Morfil had been a diligent and loyal subordinate, but he lacked Irion's intrepid nature. Besides, he was now obliged to the duties of the highest order, whereas Irion was practically a nomad from the lower. It was time for something new. Through Irion, I was free.

As the first rains splashed off my hood, I laughed as ghouls do. I was alive again, and the pitter-patter on my tongue was as sweet as bliss itself. It was time to pay my respects to the wondrous House of Rogaire. I marched toward the Thunder Bustle, through the flower-adorned precincts of the wealthier tombs.

Seasmil's Tale

I: We All Arrive at the Morgue Somehow

I ENJOY MY WORK. It's an occupation I'm not surprised I ended up in, although it was not my original dream. But that's the case with every man who holds down an honest wage. I work at the Nilghorde Pauper Morgue, where endless droves of vagrants are flopped out of carts and off horse backs to land on my table. With me they all end. It's a brief inspection really, well that and some paperwork, as per a severely outdated policy that began in the Years of Peace, when the red, scale mail, sabers, and spears of the Conqueror's soldiers became the blue, chainmail, sabers, and clubs of the Metropolitan Ward.

After initial duties, the corpses are usually tossed down into the Pauper Vault, the mass grave of our fair city. My work is not limited to the homeless, of course, for there are many orphans and prostitutes. There is even the occasional victim of a crime of passion, one whose aggressor possessed the quick wit to pay off one of my bosses. I can safely say I've seen every level of our opulent society on my table at some point or another.

Now, as I toil among the dead, the statues of Do-Gooder's Row are finished, polished weekly by working parties sent from the Municipal Dungeon. Never one to forgo the juices of irony, tonight's assignment was brought to me from the vast confines of this Row. These poor sots killed each other over a damned mule cart. A mule cart! All five of them. Skewered and heads busted over life's wares and trinkets—though such wares and trinkets feed the desperate gullet, as I used to know all too well. Snier also knew this. I'll get to him later. He is, or, I've grown to worry, *was* one of the wiliest men ever to be met in Nilghorde—and that is no small feat, considering my home's rather well-deserved reputation for what I'd once heard coined "pleasant predation." I reckon that, if he would have slipped into this fiasco, Snier would have picked these dead men clean before the first horse hoof had echoed. But who knows where some end up, especially those prone to the ebb and flow like flotsam.

Ready for the table, all ten eyes have curiously found a way to look into one another. Flopped off a Ward cart to form a crude ring on my floor, Somyellia would have likely been able to summon some obedient demon straight up from its center.

And I must say, before embarking on this tale of magic and murder, I think this ring of dead men is fitting. An apt metaphor, if you will. Yes, morticians *can* be as lettered as they are solitary. The metaphor in that what lies ahead is more than just corpses on floors, but different people—characters on this grand macabre stage—different angles to be presented. Some would say it's the only way. Even time itself can become angular, for what is time to the dead? For this is the province we now call Rehleia, and most of us are inescapably linked, even if some will never know it.

I can't impress that, this *linkage*, enough. Leading me, if you are one unfamiliar with our ways, to beg for what you may call some pre-tale forgiveness.

Rehleian tales are often told by a choir of orators. Some in your standard harmony; others, calculated step-overs as if competing for stardom and the license to history. These dead men here, my work tonight: The Ward did say there were others, the stronger ones, the ones with knife-skills and a wolf's temper, those who lived, and ran off with hands full as law enforcement rained down upon the dead and dying. Based on the tattooing, and choice of rags signifying to us locals what district they scoundrel'd out of, these men here were unacquainted, perhaps happenstance and hunger propelling their feet to the base of those standing tall on Do-Gooder's Row. Yet they would be so eternally connected. Please remember this, the web and how the spiders tell of it, as it is our way, in the city of Nilghorde, all of Rehleia, and I'd be willing to bet a coin or two throughout all Mulgara.

It is convenient last night's bloodbath allows me to mention Do-Gooder's Row. When its knees or eyes were chiseled free from the towering lines of dull white, these moments have served as time-keeping devices for us Rehleians. The chiseling began the day our Years of Peace were declared. And much like my own life, happenings and fortunes have often been remembered by what stage the statues were in when life gave us our surprises.

These days, champions like Zaderyn Fover, a citizen who dove into the Black Tongue only to be carried off by its currents while trying to save a drowning child, shine bright and polished. But much of my tale will pull us back, back when the statues were but ugly rectangles crowned with faces and shoulders tortured by marble tumors.

###

MY NAME IS SEASMIL Oleugsby. Most would say I am a large man. I'd concur; made from the heavy lifting, but not solely due to all the bodies. When I am lifting, my hair is tied in a ponytail; black hair, though like the many scars on my skin, it wasn't always that way.

I was named after my great-grandfather, who led a charge on a camp of cannibal pirates off the coast of Suela. His name grew to legendary status, despite a rather gruesome end. He and his company were roasted alive in suits of hardened clay. Apparently there is a holiday in that idol-worshipping land that still mimics all of this. A ragged sailor once told how the women rub their clitorises on the face of the still-screaming meal to be. I often wondered if my ancestor had suffered this intriguing punishment, and if he had felt a final delight before the world went dark. It was a neglected portrait that hung from a wall during my youth that told me from him I'd inherited the Oleugsby menace: flat forehead, deep-set eyes, and a square jaw.

I was born and raised in Nilghorde; in the Templeton District to be exact, designated for the martial servicemen and their families. We were on an edge of the city, where the farthest line of homes faced a great forest. Templeton was a sturdy square, once cut from the forest and sown on the Nilghorde quilt. Inside our heavily patrolled borders sat the steep-roofed stone houses surrounded by all you'd expect to see in the farmlands.

And I do mean heavily patrolled. Despite it being a district in Nilghorde, there was little crime. Most of the watchmen and the Metropolitan Ward lived there. They hadn't busted heads all over this land to allow swarms of riffraff to spill into their own domiciles. But in the earlier days, when the Conqueror was waging war and the future-wardsmen were his soldiers, Templeton was a place where fathers were gone most of the year, leaving children to be raised by elder siblings or their promiscuous mothers.

I was an only child, but that was just fine by me. From the beginning, I'd always fallen deep into the joys of solitude and imaginary friends. These playmates inhabited holes in trees and pawed the floor under my bed. By the time I was catching up to the height of my mother, I had shed any interest in sports or games played out in the streets.

That, though, wasn't from being alone too much—as Mother quibbled at times. I'd discovered the world of science. I begged

Mother for an alchemy set. After much whining and mutinies at the dinner table, she caved and brought me a little wooden box. It wasn't just filled with mineral pouches, corked vials, and tiny cutting tools—it bore wonder. In my hands were the keys to the doors of the natural world.

The little box became my obsession. The few friends who still lingered about stopped knocking on our door. Mother's pleas to go outside and play eventually stopped too. Far less gratifying, imaginary friends turned to dust. One by one, faint screams, audible to my ears alone, and then there were only shadows. I particularly remember the elf in the old elm on the edge of Templeton Park. He sat crouching in the canopy, silent as always. His stare haunted me for a long time. Disapproving of me leaving the mists of fairyland for pragmatism was certainly understandable. But it also couldn't be stopped.

I eventually focused on the visceral endeavors and varied my experiments greatly, from futile attempts at tracking stars to more enjoyable branches dealing with the inner workings of anything I could either trap, scavenge, or lure with meat.

II: Into Cellars

SEASMIL," I OFTEN HAVE to tell myself. "If you are going to go into the backstory, be sure not to leave out the most important stuff." For backstory is merely useful for jutting us forward into that great, mysterious yonder. And I should know this, being I've spent more nights falling through book's pages than your average paid scholar. With this bit in mind, telling my tale would be a wide chasm from thorough if I failed to tell of my father, in his entirety, as is best known to me.

No, not some Ordrid—though you may have anticipated such a revelation due to, among other things, my habits and choice of work.

No, my father was Augnor Olcugsby, a cavalryman in the notorious regiment Swift Saber. The SS was a highly deployed unit under the Conqueror himself, and subsequently, I don't have any recollection of my father in the house amid my earliest years. Despite his absence, we did not struggle. Charges and pillages accumulated, bringing back chest upon chest of jewels and coin.

My father was a beast of a man, a stone golem with legs like unhewn trees, and a neck like an oxen in the farmlands where Mother had come out of.

The first memory I can muster was of him telling Mother a spirited story. With the smell of the saddle still lingering, he recounted riding through the farmlands of Serabandantilith and mowing the villagers down like grass. I didn't hear the whole tale, and time has a way of inflating and deflating the sanctity of memory, but I do remember a comparison of some people to the height of our kitchen cupboard. I was eye level with the cupboard myself back then and tried to make sense of how men were so small in other lands. As was her nature, or at least her developed one, Mother listened half-heartedly, trying multiple times in vain to clue Father in that I was listening, and do so without infuriating him.

Whether Father was riding the famed memory of his grand-father, or was an exemplary soldier, or a combination of the two, I do not know, but he'd embarked on a career in which he was being groomed for a lofty and prestigious rank. Chief Horseman perhaps, or maybe a lower seat in the Office of Scepters when his ruthlessness left the saber and moved to an inkwell. All I know is, wherever he was slotted to go came to a sudden and unmovable halt when I was about ten.

We never really knew where he was or when he'd be returning. There were the wives meetings, where the senior crone married to some military relic long overdue for retirement would disseminate the latest news through scroll and lecture. Mother hated those. In one of her more humorous moments, she reenacted how catty they all were and how without delay the meetings would degrade to drunk clucking hens gossiping over which watchmen was the most endowed and notes on his availability.

So, it's no surprise to me now that one fateful winter, when Father was supposed to be on the forefront of some vague campaign, he was attending to the wife of a field grade commander in his SS.

We found out weeks after. Father had returned home a wretch, reluctantly telling Mother that he was done deploying due to "some arbitrary insubordination." For all the stolen gold in the Thunder Bustle, I couldn't fathom why Mother didn't tear the house apart and leave him emasculated after he had fallen asleep. She took it on the chin and seemed to recover back to her dismal role as housewife to the once-great warrior. You would have barely noticed anything at all, save the additional silence at the table and the lines in her face that had deepened. But hindsight is an unchained dragon, cruel but liberated. I know now why Mother remained in that house in Templeton.

Despite a heated debate among his superiors, Father was allowed to retain a paying position. As a man it occurred to me maybe it was his greatest detractors who gleefully fought for this altered retention. Demoted to a stable master for one of the SS garrisons, our once healthy stock of horses were sold off, their mountain of feed abandoned to mottle with the fungi that I examined and the vermin that I caught.

Most of the time, Father would bring his work home with him—we certainly had the room in the stables. Mother once whispered he was too embarrassed to be seen in his billet by his former brethren.

One of the few reasons he wasn't pulled apart by a departing pair of Saber warhorses was he'd saved the life of an esteemed officer. At the time Father's infidelities were being exposed, this officer had climbed to the seat of Vice Chief Horseman and had enough clout to muffle the baying of the scorned husband. Although the Vice Chief's influence spared my father, the same could not be said for his loose-ring-bearing mistress, whose corpse dangled on the Tower of the Waning Moon for a season of crows and maggots.

This Vice Chief's generosity bore our family other gifts too. Soon after the SS returned from the deployment where Father had saved his life, he came to our home one evening for a dinner. And not any ordinary dinner. Mother had banged around in the kitchen almost as frantic as she did over her wardrobe, ending it stuffed in a dress never to be seen again, and in front of a meal so large my boyish brain anticipated the Conqueror's entire army.

He was a noble-looker, the type whose gray feathered hair and blue eyes made you wonder why he'd ever signed on to shit next to men with blade wounds stitched by other lugs; squatting over the same trench, dug by men for whose wounds there was no fixing. He left us with a chest that *chunked* when it hit the floor, and he sang Father's praises until the night drew me weary. Right before he departed, he brought me from his carriage a baby lamb, black as midnight. My best guesses were it was either some custom of warrior etiquette—a gesture of giving life to the seed of the man who saved his—or a grand display of appreciation for Mother's cooking.

Though I was informed of every glorious detail, it was still hard not to wonder if Father had really dashed into that ambush to save him not for duty or for that brotherly love soldier-types love to go on about, but rather to quench a bloodlust. Truth is, that Vice Chief knew my father in a way I never did. I would be false to not say that a lifetime ago I wished to see this man, to sit on his knee and partake in his celebrations, to wear his giant helmet and be tossed in the air. Bruises simply meant I received something different.

My experiments on our neighbor's cat brought a particular salvo, and the manner in which I returned the feline only heated the beating. Around that time, stable work lost a lot of its demand. To fill the gap, Father took an avid interest in denouncing my hopes and daily endeavors. That damn cat was all it took. The alchemy kit was pried from my hands, only to be shoved against my chest a moment later. I wept without restraint when I was ordered to break all the vials. Afterward I assumed the usual stance and held firewood above my head until my shoulders screamed. Somewhere in this memory I recited the piece of martial jingle

I'd recite a thousand times: the SS creed. As an adult my mind has shunted all but two stanzas:

One rider, ten riders, or riders score
Through pain, through cold, through plain, through moor

I don't think he ever planned for me to be a warrior, and if he did, he surely changed his mind after his demotion. "Bunch of damn beggars in armor," he'd say. "Lousy mob whores praising the cowardly; worshipped those that pass out bread instead of the blade."

This, of course, worked to my benefit. The rank and file could march off our land's tallest cliff for all I cared. Like most children in Templeton, I enjoyed a comprehensive education, poring over sonnets and rattling an abacus with a series of tutors—maybe even more so, since no son of Augnor would wear armor in peacetime. My favorite subject was unsurprisingly biology, and it may have been boyish defiance, but Father's classic *soldier's disdain* for the arts and academia only strengthened my resolve to not only be a man of science but a medical doctor. So what if my tastes were a little unorthodox from the start?

With funding procured from Mother's undergarments drawer, which had been procured from Father's last heavy chest, I built an upgraded version of my laboratory—this time in the cobweb-infested cellar of our most vacated and dilapidated barn. Once I was sure the ogre who stalked my waking life was unaware of operational headquarters, I continued to explore the governing of all life-forms that I could drag through the candlelight.

Around the time when hair began to sprout in new places, I snuck out one night and penetrated deep into the city. I scurried through alleys. At the risk of abduction or worse, I finally found what I was searching for outside the back of a noisy brothel. It was soft, pink, and barely dead. I brought it home and down into the cellar. It was the first of its kind, but surely not the last.

III: Seasmil and Somyellia

L EADING MINDS SAY ALL this gods talk is nonsense," my old tutor used to say. "Tubes and muck are we."

One of many in a long line of educators that ran screaming from our home, this tutor had been a student himself. The Institute of Human Sciences, Rehleia's premier medical school, was placed on a Nilghorde hill like some jaded royalty. More than just eliminative materialism, I learned from this scholar that the Institute did all sorts of fascinating studies in its grand halls. The true tome of treasure came the day he brought me an old course book of his. I hid it deep in the cellar, behind a skull of a large dog and several jars of entrails from woodland fauna. The findings within the book were a stream of wonder. And soon a river.

I have been accused of being a callous man, solitary and apathetic to the plight of others, but I can say that if that is so, that I wasn't always. This tutor had been warned by Father, backed against a wall in our den, random sharp object to his neck, not to encourage my peculiarness and stick to the curriculum. When a distant neighbor called upon our door to ask if we'd seen her dog, not only did I receive a staunch one, but the best teacher I ever had collected his last payment with the helpful removal of his front row of teeth.

Mother pleaded my innocence, even drumming up the courage to compare unfounded accusations made by the SS at Father's expense. In truth, part of that neighbor's pet hid my begifted course book. My guilt in that matter served no purpose to surface.

Now it must be understood, this lamb placed in my arms by the Vice Chief was also slotted for the operating table. I wanted to see if it could survive with a transfusion of my own blood. The experiment of course presented itself while I was reading one of the studies. The Institute had run a lengthy trial, placing vats of murderer blood from the Municipal Dungeon into orphans' arms. Most of the orphans died before transfusion, but a few strong specimens survived. The damn rainwater ruined the last several pages, but I imagined the spectacular transformation of these test subjects in their cages: street children screaming through the bars with eyes of predation, walking among the caged viewing areas while pumping the blood of cutthroats. I didn't have the resources needed for full replication, but a lamb wasn't bad.

I'd spent a week or so tactfully letting my blood, being sure to avoid the constant threat of discovery and cataclysmic reaction from my parents. Then the "Day of the Lamb," as I'd come to call it, finally arrived. Enough blood was stored, and Father was heavily asleep from a full day of the stable.

I laugh now at the ruthless ambition. Although cursedly naïve at the time, as we all must be, I am proud of who I was at such a young age. The story was already concocted: wolves stole the lamb. And I was going to use the blood I drained from it to make room for my own and paint a believable scene of carnage.

Down in the cellar, to optimize my sight, I placed candles in the shape of a triangle. In this triangle's center was a low table that I laid the lamb on. I tied down a front leg, but when I reached for the other, chaos erupted.

We fought like pit fighters. A mad chase around the table sent the transfusion gear into every nook and cranny. My jar became a half-congealed explosion. He stayed me with a rear kick to the jaw and when the lights went away I felt pure nausea.

At the end of it, we were covered in sappy blood, both panting. My heart beat harder at the thought that Father may have heard. Equally, I imagine, the lamb was terrified of some determined lad, with rope in hand at the opposite end of an unpleasant cellar.

It was then I looked into those black-jeweled eyes. Maybe I was being melodramatic then, and maybe I am a bit still, but this thing had the courage to fight off his attacker—like a drunken banshee— whereas I took my beatings without recourse. I'd killed hundreds of rats, snakes, cats, and dogs who put up less of a fight. It is hard for someone who dwells in the company of people and song to understand, but I felt a closeness with this creature that was beyond that of normal explanation. Up until then I hadn't named him, but right then he became Celly. A childish, campy, spondee of a name, sure, but it signified the cellar, where I met my best friend and where, I still believe, two spirits connected.

We emerged out onto the floor of the barn. Gigantic horses glared with an oppressive over-watch. We washed at the well, and I returned him to his corral. Sneaking back inside I breathed a sigh of relief, hearing snores that would humble a bear.

After that night, Celly and I were inseparable. He followed me on my long walks through the shores of the wood-line, where I showed him all the snares and pitfalls that I used to capture wide-eyed shriekers. I'd sneak him in the house sometimes, and he would sleep next to me in bed. His smell, long-lasting, I remedied with heavy incense and constantly cracked windows. He and I both grew in stature, and we spent many a summer night sitting on the floor of the cellar, one reading to the other.

###

A NIGHT IN THE late spring I heard strange noises from our kitchen. It was a faint rustling, followed by a sound that reminded me of the cracking of firewood. And after that nothing more.

At the time, a banishment to my bedroom for some shortcoming prohibited me from investigating any further. The next morning I awoke to Father screaming. That was nothing particularly unusual, except this time there rang a unique desperation. I ran out to see him on his knees, back toward me. He held Mother, dead as dead could be. The rope hung without motion, tied to a rafter where our kitchen met the den.

The thought of her watching over me in some a state of... *unbeing* the prior night sparked the hair on my arms.

Her face showed the full effects, and her neck I could not bear.

I must have let out a small yelp, because there was a moment where Father turned to me. He had the look of a painting made by a decadent and angry artist. He hadn't cried, or at least I hadn't heard him, but his eyes were red, and not the usual shade.

Mother was buried in the Ansul of Chapwyn Cemetery. We couldn't get one of their priests to do the service, due to some stipulation about suicide. This sent Father into a wailing rage, which deepened the sense of weight and sadness that only the family of a suicide can tell.

Father was able to convince a martial priest from the SS to come out. Formerly delegated to sprinkling incense on brand-new war dead, he waved his hands and saw her into the dirt. Word had passed through the ranks, and it was the only time I got to see a dressed array of some of my father's brothers-in-arms. I saw men whom I didn't know console him in ways I'd wished then that I was able.

We rode back home, me behind him on the notch of a one-man saddle. I put my arms around his abdomen, a place that was once as hard as mountain stone, now turned to gut. I retracted them and decided to take my chances with a slipping grip of the saddle blanket.

THE TIMES IMMEDIATELY AFTER Mother's characteristic exit were filled with an even greater silence at home. Well, silence between the remnants of the family more like—taking into account the tarts with more legs than years left on earth who frequented the place. Abysmal void at the dinner table followed by broken glasses, head-tilt feminine laughter, and sex made for a house better fit for a madman.

It took Father no effort to find these women, and I surmised that at least one of them contributed to my mother's suicide—maybe all of them. Years prior, I guess there would have been some hatred for my mother. Why couldn't she have informed me of her discovery, and why couldn't we have just left? But coin and shelter are not just given, and past the mere pragmatics, I also know how some are slaves to their own omissions, and I never pondered why there wasn't a note.

To separate myself from the clamor that had become home, I delved deeper into my projects and fought with all my might not to acknowledge my budding interest in Father's ill-gotten company. Many a time, a dissection was halted to ponder the contents under a silk black dress.

One evening a rotten carriage, pulled by a set of mares looking just as bad, brought three women to our door. When they stepped out I was dizzied by the heavy sway of the redheaded leader's breasts. The other two were quite young, close enough to my own age, but all were equally dressed for their trade.

There was a sickening wave of emotions for my father right then. Disgust—how could you disgrace your dead wife's bed with the juices of women whose names you wouldn't remember in the morrow? Envy—how utterly enthralling these women were, and then how I would have joined my cold mother for a chance just to feel their warm embrace.

I ran off to my cellar, seeing it as this ridiculous hiding place for bones. Weeping with my face in my hands helped; taking breaks only to—well. One night while spying on Father through a bedroom window, I saw two of his voluptuous companions do to him, one hand on top of the other, what I did furiously and frequently to break up the crying.

Hours must have passed before I emerged, for it was dark and the wind licked cold. As I walked up to our side door, it swung open, almost toppling me over. The three women filed out in their slightly rearranged attire. The night did not conceal the return of the redhead's jiggle, a sight that sent my soul wailing back into the cellar.

This time, however, before I could make my retreat, one of the young ones thwarted me. By the light of the moon and a street lamp I saw her: fair skinned, golden-eyed. Her hair was the color of dew on lilies, which she wore in braids that ended at the crack of a backside I already held visions of. Perky breasts exposed their contours under an evilly cut garment, and above them were eyelashes that batted at me.

"Hi," she said as if talking to someone capable of speech. "You're Augy's boy?"

"By blood," I managed to squeak out, utterly amazed at my own response.

I don't know if it was because we were both standing as still as Lirelet statues, or if it was because I was still mouthing *by blood* to myself in half-astonishment, but I didn't hear their ride pull up. It was her glance that notified me. Once pulled out of whatever jackassery I was surely swirling around in, I heard the full rattling of the carriage and smelled the low-burning lamps affixed to its mean wooden face.

"Time we're off, Somyellia," the endowed leader confirmed. The motherly tone wasn't lost on me—both in its oddity and its ability to soothe—as she and the other pranced down our wooden steps. This time I didn't stare at her tits. It was as if she never had them.

Somyellia, as she was called, looked at me, tilted her head, bit her bottom lip.

"I...I can take her home," I said.

"I don't know, young master," said the ranking mistress.

"Come now, Morlia," Somyellia said to her. "Deny such a strapping youngling?"

"Silence, Morlia," wedged a croaking voice from the carriage. "You want her, it's twenty silver more. She'll be back by morning." The words ran up my spine like a dry tongue.

"I have it," I found myself saying.

"Somyellia," spoke the carriage, "come back with the money."

As the carriage departed, she looked more like a girl playing dress-up than one of *Augy's* whores. But she wasn't playing anything. She had cavorted and hiked her legs up in palaces and mansions all throughout Nilghorde—perhaps all Rehleia—perhaps beyond our watery borders. She'd bounced atop soldierly bodies. She'd escorted the unrepentantly wealthy, on her hands and knees above pits of decorated hunting cats and amid silk and gold. I was a whelp, and she had either found an appeal in my innocence or had much more devious plans in store.

Under a swollen moon I meandered. Her lip was bit again, and to my terror I'd once more lost my powers of speech. Pollen from nearby gardens filled our noses, and if it weren't for the decay on my clothes we would have looked like characters right out of the *Poems of the Classics*. Wind ran around our bodies, and the moon peered down upon its children.

"What is your name?" she said.

"Seasmil."

"That's an unusual name. What does it mean?"

"I—I don't really know," I said. She was beautiful *and* thought-provoking! "Never thought about it much. I was named after a relative. Does yours mean something?" While sunk in self-consciousness, I shifted my attention as best as I could from the ornaments adorning her to thoroughly digging a small hole in front of me with the toe of my boot.

"Of course," she popped. "All who are kin to Maecidion the Virulent possess names with direct meaning."

"What?"

"Mine means *daughter of the sleeping demon*," she said in the manner of a small child announcing their alignment with a favored pit fighter, flag in hand. She giggled, and her big gold eyes flashed. "Why are you covered in all that filth?"

"Oh, no I was—do you want to see something?"

Maybe it was because my dismal lab was the only thing I could claim in the whole world as my own. Or maybe it was because she had looked at me with the eyes of a woman who may have really bore the meaning of her name.

She nodded, and with her hand in mine, I escorted her to my dark cellar of experiments, where I hungered for an experiment of a different kind.

As with many men's first, I was in a state of euphoric confusion. Starting things off was a showing of human skulls. The stall tactic was excruciation itself, made only greater when they all found a way to tumble out of my fumbling arms. Aside from the stock insecurities of adolescence, the aroma of my lab—a thing I'd grown so accustomed to that my nose could almost omit decay—burst into my face as if it were the first time ever smelling a corpse. Surely, she would take flight up my stairs, this creature sitting on a table so covered in macabre. Most women would have stopped at the cellar door, yet she began to undress in the stench and shadow.

Never taking her eyes off of me, she undressed as she had so many times before.

Her buttocks rested on the edge of the table. Her dress was shed with the flick of a leg. Her arms were locked at the elbow, hands gripping the edge. Her mouth hung open, bee-stung lips moist and shining in the candlelight.

The candlelight itself, a thing between those shelves and pillars as familiar to me as portraits on a wall. On this night, though, the light gave birth to shapes that danced as if spectators to an enchantress... and me, standing awkwardly with a handful of skulls.

She curled a finger: *come hither*. I dropped the skulls again. My eyes were locked on a soft and sideways grimace. A faint patch of hair above it wanted to be smelled, and I walked closer, into the gap that her legs had made.

She gripped the back of my head with one hand and my small boyish buttocks with the other. "Show me you're your father's son," she said, showing her teeth. As she pulled me closer I felt like an animal caught in one of my snares—almost.

Our lips met, and she had my trousers off and my horned member grasped before I could even realize her perfume didn't overwhelm the odors that I'd momentarily forgotten. A cacophony of little pops and squishes erupted when I pressed her back against the table. I thought she was going to go berserk, but to my amazement, and to my delight, she smiled. We rolled off the table and onto the floor.

When our needs had been met, we stood up and looked at the other. She was still smiling; that girly side of hers having returned, save for the fact that she now looked like a recently feasted ghoul. I must have been a sight to see too, relishing the mixture of sex and death that was to become my adult life.

After we emerged, I took her to meet Celly, whom she endeared with petting and rubbed her face against with shut-eyed kisses. She soon informed me of the whereabouts of her unsavory quarters, and told me not to worry about the silver. I did not question her.

It was time to go.

Filled with the empowerment of sexual knowing, and drugged with the aroma of rot and her strong perfume, I stole one of my father's horses.

We sprung forth into the air. Wolves from the forest howled as we galloped out of the Templeton District, always on the lookout for a roving patrol. We were bound for the deformed, cobbled alleys that formed the crime-ridden Thunder Bustle District, where you were as likely to bump into a sorcerer weaving their outlawed magic as you were to lose your purse.

As we rode, she clutched my waist, buildings and landmarks of the city flying by. Our route went from dirt to the *clickity-clack* of cobblestones. Eyes peered out, lurking behind glass windows that never opened. We avoided the shadowy figures that approached us when I paused at an intersection for Somyellia to get her bearings. The salt smell thickened. Except for the horse underneath us, we were the only living things for the last leg of our journey.

We arrived at the backside of an old warehouse busy leaning into the sea. It was a block of wet black, grayed at the edges by some source of light. At the door were the ugliest men I had ever seen. Armed with pikes, their scars came either from disastrous afflictions of acne or battling fierce beasts with dispositions for biting.

"This is it, Seasmil," Somyellia said with a calmness that had no place there. "Thank you for the ride."

She walked up a series of waterlogged steps to the guardsmen, and whispered something in one's ear that was met with a nod. Turning to face me, she looked like a thing of beauty who had chosen to give up beauty for darker delights, but whose attraction had yet to wither. Her hair now an unkempt mess of twists and shoots, she smiled and waved and disappeared through a doorway to a place that I wanted to follow at the expense of my very soul.

The brief introspection was cut short when a blood-wrenching scream erupted deep in the alleys, followed by a mob of hurried feet.

I was now again the boy from Templeton, on his father's stolen horse, without a weapon or a guide. I proceeded to fly through the wormy spaces, between buildings all appearing abandoned. Trying to remember the direction in which we had come, and later avoiding the shaking lanterns of surely pursuing sentries, I made it back to the barn before sunrise.

I tended to the horse and agonized over the minute details of the gear, mostly what side of any particular piece was facing the wall and what wasn't. But more than that, I agonized about *her*. Would I ever see her again?

Boys shedding their innocence for the more nefarious practices of adolescence is the source of ocean's worth of poetry. My towering escapade with Somyellia was no exception. Only such an encounter could intoxicate me enough to run off with one of Father's horses. Carrying out my clandestine venture undetected only provoked my sense of achievement. Although doing so far too young for the approval of the bland and proper, I had peeked into the vault of teeming secrets that no book or vial could contain or explain. I was hooked, and I found myself a terrible thirst in a raging storm.

At the expense of my bungling studies, I set my eyes on that dancing, warm flesh. An addled burrow of Nilghorde meant nothing. I was the second Seasmil; trapper of teethed mites, owner of skulls, avoider of the Ward, and one whose vigor listened not to the gray and cockless distracters of recourse or consequence.

Father had taken an even more nominal interest in my happenings. An increased workload and a growing penchant for the bottle carried him off into an advantageous solitude. I could stay in my lab for a full day and night, just to emerge for some wonted ramble of housework to be done. I was far past the days of subtle paternal want and hopes. Neglect was my ally. As long as my chores were done, my scholarly work fulfilled, and my changing face occasionally seen, I was free, and my loins would find their quenching, even if it meant the coming of terror.

And such quenching mandated that I did indeed see her again. On the backs of stolen horses, Somyellia and I rode to new places to sow oats and memories alike, many lost now like rain in the sea. I became well versed in the ways of women. For she would on occasion nestle away one of her coworkers, and for my pleasant discovery they'd execute carefully rehearsed acts on my body, often tied down and blindfolded. Her expertise from her employment left me mesmerized and trembling, always outdoing herself with random accessories of opium, leather, or blood.

We chased moonlight, dancing wickedly behind tall graves before defiling them with human juices. She showed me the black arts of her Ordrid kind, explaining she'd shown promise in curses. I gave her animal hearts with Mother's few remaining jewels deep in the tough muscles.

I became somewhat of an expert in avoiding the black-drabbed ruffians en route to acquire her: a toss of silver here, a swift gallop over a rotten fence. I declare, I learned more about the Thunder Bustle, and remained uncut, than the most resourceful local. I became a most regular of irregular sights in front of that ogre-guarded door. Once she was wrapped around me, like the plague dressed in silk and wolf's fur, we would disappear into the smoke, shadow and brick maze to some predestined bungalow. Alone, we'd commence our carnal rites, and not the howling of the forest wolves or roaring of the sea could drown our ecstasy.

We both found a happiness that was all our own. When her work bid her away, I would pass the time with half-hearted dissections and long walks with Celly.

#

CELLY—OR LORD CELLURZGA, AS Somyellia sometimes insisted, supposedly paying homage to one of her Ordrid ancestors whose royal feet, if left too long on wood, revealed seared hoofprints— grew into a beautiful hoofed beast. Our voyages through the forest were done in the contented silence that romance books always fawn on about. And maybe I'm guilty of wordy romancing too, as you may have already nocked that critic's arrow. But this silence was pristine, interrupted only by the occasional predator that met staff and stone, and a lone stumble into our land's reigning religion: a rural Chapwyn encampment.

I was lured one day by moans I believe belonged to a wounded deer in a tabernacle of young pine. The moans of such a deer struck by some woodland malady became a circle of men, no more than a handful, wrapped in the same filth-white garb as the tabernacle's roof. They were all kneeling, bent so far forward one fell over into the dirt. In the center stood a priest, in cleaner sheets and holding an unspooled scroll in one hand and an uprooted plant in the other. Both the scroll and plant lowered as he watched Celly, myself, and my fang-nicked staff descend the slope of bramble and ferns.

"He who walketh with Animal as Man is either thy steward of sentience or Animal himself." The Chapwyn priest wasn't reading from his dirty old scroll, but that didn't mean the obscure verse hadn't come right from the vellum. Lack of familiarity with this particular passage—any particular passage unsheathed at random— perhaps was the one thing I shared in common with the lay, scroll-thumping Chapwynite.

The verse lingered on the leader's face, emaciated and worn like ship wood, and the rest had either risen or turned to behold the object in question. I heard Celly's hooves, curious and cautious as they clopped down on wet leaves. Coming up against my thigh, my freehand found a good patch of his wool to grab and rest in.

Animals that you don't kill can smile, I swear to you. Celly's made the warmer of the parishioners giggle.

"Didn't mean to interrupt," I said, eyeing the slosh of heavy-boot trails that led back to somewhere in Nilghorde. I was now close enough to this rustic communion to knock a kneeler over with the muddy end of my staff. Beyond them, wooden bowls made an inner ring around the priest's feet. In them were what appeared to be equal dispersings of water, bread, hand axes, and shit. "Didn't know this was—"

"An intruder," the priest fired, "on Tersiona's faithful hath only strayed from his own wander and intruded on only that which hath been seen before he beeth born unto the world."

It may have been them rising in unison that backed me. My staff would've dispatched them with a few hard swings, but religious synchronization was a human convention new to me.

"He beeth no shepherd!" a voice shouted. "Beware those who giveth false witness, their…their sheep are black as their souls, those damned."

My foothold on the slope behind me ceased their advance.

"Maenoch," sighed the priest. "Forty parthings and reread the blessed scripture: those who giveth false witness *for their souls are black and damn those sheep who stay their own vigilance.*"

Maenoch hiked up his rags and began the prescribed calisthenics. Long before the fortieth hop, he gave me a malicious look, one probably later seeing him fit for Ansul's True, the martial arm of their sprawling church, populated by the militant-chaste whose final initiation was rumored to be self-inflicted castration.

"Come see us again sometime," the priest solicited, reaffirming his grip on his accessories and sounding for the first time like a man born in my century. We both turned wearing our own versions of an awkward smile. Their practice recommenced and I climbed back toward Templeton. Before I went over the crest I overheard the gist of the sermon I'd interrupted: the intrinsic good of sharing.

What a coincidence, for I didn't mind sharing Somyellia—which may surprise you if you are from Oxghorde or won't bury a lady because she hung herself. But I found her profession a quaint enterprise that only made me want her more by the hour. I had only found discord with her livelihood on one occasion.

I'd watched the rotten carriage pull up one evening, expecting the usual gaggle of tarts to file out. To my horror I watched Somyellia exit. I saw her scan to see if I were around, and saw her relief when she perceived that I wasn't.

For reasons of sheer mercy my mind has precluded any re-hashing the events from that evening, but I recall being beside myself with the sharpest type of grief. Outside Father's window I stood, biting down deep into my fists.

Our favorite meeting place was an abandoned house. It was the last home in a row, all overlooking City Cemetery. While Nilghorde was peppered with quaint little graveyards, privately owned and surrounded by high flinty walls, the city held three major ones. Besides City Cemetery, there was Whisperer's Plain and the Ansul of Chapwyn Cemetery, that last one not only holding my mother, but a virtual underground hive of the religious, the uppity, and the municipal who'd opted not to spend eternity near those who they'd ruled. City Cemetery, the colossus, stretched the farthest and the fullest. For the nights we'd float over its stones, I would leave alone the stealing of horses and make it on foot. Walking there was no short journey, and my legs after a time started taking the shape of my father's kind.

The abandoned house looked like a slight breeze would topple it. Only the cobwebs and rat shit glued the eaten frame together. Good thing those components were in such abundance. A witchy roof was still clad with a few shingles, all deeply warped from years of sun and bombarding rain. Crows made home the exposed rafters, and from a caved-in wall on the second floor, we would sit and view the silent resting place for many of the city's denizens whose families didn't possess the money to bury them with class.

We would stay the night, small fire lit in a bronze urn she'd plucked off a tomb. I loved the sort of mischievous unlife that came to shape below us, in the tiny hours of the morning where the world's shores seemed to rub against some other place. Holding Somyellia in my arms, fire to my back, I found myself longing for that place.

###

I AWOKE, GRABBING FOR my knife. "Can't fool you," Somyellia larked. Years navigating the Bustle does bear fruit. She was on the edge of our mat with a bag on her lap. Her hair always took on a cooked straw effect in the morning, before mirrors and little pink jars and her ritual of locking herself in powder rooms. This game of hers, moving my knife while I slept, brought her more mirth than a seat at the front of a good theatre. She said she loved seeing the "whip and flash" of how I snatched it, and how I never missed, whether moved from our left side to our right, or stuck in the floor behind my head. For me it only brought a jolt to the heart and a lump in my throat, but it also woke me as absolute as Pelat coffee. Convincing myself this was the reason for her dropping loose boards or screaming in my ear helped me fight back a second reflex that sometimes came after I'd wrapped my fingers around the handle.

Rubbing the sleep from my eyes, the knife was tossed and I fell back into my sheets. "I better return all this leather," Somyellia said to herself with a yawn. Looking across my chest and between my feet, familiar portions of last night's ensemble were sticking out from her bag. There was a cool breeze, and angry crows squawked somewhere in the rafters. "Or have my hands dipped in oil."

"Would they even notice?" I said.

"I am *so* hungry. Do we have anything left?"

"No," I said, rolling onto my side.

"Oh. No bother, I'm going to pick up some things on the way."

"See you tonight?"

"Not tonight. There's some bachelor party for a Lotgard that starts at dusk and is going to last for three days."

"Yeah, I need to go home anyway," I said, having learned well to mask these mild disappointments.

"Well," she exhaled in a patronizing tone she'd come to perfect, "I promise to meet you here as soon as the festivities end," tickling my exposed side, "my beast."

We departed with a kiss. She turned to go back to her nest, as I began the long walk back.

The sun came out late but made up for its tardiness. By the time I stepped onto the first dirt road, I was sweating in the gleam. I rounded a bend that I had rounded many times before, viewing the red-topped roof of The Great Fuckity House of Oleugsby.

Now, when I tell you that I felt something was *off*, I don't mean that under the perfect reflection of memories retold. I don't mean to say that looking back I felt something was wrong merely by knowing what happened next. As I met the wooden fence that separated our yard from the road, there was a cold in my gut.

The cellar? He had found my lab! My first impulse was of him walking past its door. Maybe I had meant to close it, but some arbitrary piece of rubbish kept it open just enough? Maybe he had, for some uncharacteristic reason, developed a brief curiosity about where I spent most of my days? I snuck around the side of the house, constantly examining the windows, thief-like, for any signs of life. As I approached the back, I heard a faint monotonous ring coming from his favorite barn.

"Shoeing," I said, relieved. An image I had of him hovering over my cellar door began to dissolve.

I scurried there anyway. A quick inspection revealed that all was as I'd left it. I decided to go at least take a look at Father. Not for any reason one could readily ascribe, but I couldn't place a sensation that still lingered, and I now felt wrapped in some lurid investigation.

The farrier hammer, making the usual *tinks* and *tanks*, echoed from the other side of the barn. I approached in a timid walk. Talking to him wasn't something that happened all that often, and I was already formulating my rebuttal for his most probable, stern request for some laboring assistance.

Turning the corner, I stopped at the sight before me. In a pool of his own blood lay Celly. His coal black fur was so much darker than the white skull and pinkish brain.

A wave of emotions pummeled me. He wasn't dead...and I had enough tools to repair the wound. This creature, my friend, lay in torment unattended. Sickness, yes. Guilt, that too. I felt the world spin, and some chorus of nameless mocking things sang their pale and dead incantations as I tried to breathe.

Most of all, I felt hatred. A hatred that made the world turn cold.

I was not a young man who was naïve to the presence and yields of hate. I had dwelled in a sort of darkness my whole life, and wrestled with my disconnected family at an early age and left that hope abandoned, dead in some field. The hate upon the sight this day was a treachery. When I saw that the corral gate was ajar, I put together what happened.

Celly had managed to break out. With my increased time away, he had most likely made the mistake of wandering up to Father for something as simple as a head rub. Father, busy with his stable duties, turned out to be in no mood for such troublesome interruptions. He killed Celly with one hammer blow to the head.

Behind a stable wall, sounds of work resumed. I couldn't see him, but he was close. Tools hung about me.

I snatched a hefty pick and gripped its handle. I fought the urge to look over at Celly, knowing I'd weep uncontrollably if I did. I crept to the edge of the wall, then I could fight that urge no longer. My spine bent and jerked as I wept, vomiting violent and uncontrollable little meeps.

I felt again the oaken handle in my hands. I turned toward the hammer noises; face flushed with tears, jowls open and twitching as I squeezed it, wide-eyed and beyond all reason.

I walked the way a man may right before his own execution—before the concerns of the world have left the crude carriage of flesh and bone that vessels a spirit ready for voyage.

All it would take was one committed strike. His skull would split like firewood. All I needed was for his back to be turned and his pink brain attending the last shoe it would ever contemplate.

For all his conquests, he was to be ended at the hands of his son. He deserved this, and he could be buried next to Mother, as I would surely dance in their ashes.

I turned the corner and gazed upon his back.

His head was hunkered low. Behind him I, his son, wielded a farm tool like a frontline pikeman. I always picture this through the eyes of some nonexistent spectator. That tiny moment in time haunts me, the image of us.

Killing had been an obligation of my means of obtaining animals, and some of my more risky ventures into the city bore me witness to many faces of death.

But for reasons I didn't understand, my grip loosened. I was slipping from the midnight-garbed avenger to the terrified little boy.

I found myself filled with fear—worse, indecision. I begged for my rage to return to me, and with it the strength to carry out this monumental deed.

I wondered for years what my father's reaction was when he finally turned to see a lone pick laying behind him in the beaten grass.

Without as much as a sack of grain or change of clothes, I ran away from the barn, the house, the district, my life. I ran until the dirt turned to stones and wheezed as my heart burned from exhaustion. I finally stopped at the base of my and Somyellia's abandoned house. Molested by the sweat and grime of my flight, I laid myself on its doorstep. At some point I lifted myself and slugged up the stairwell, finally lying on our animal hides. The house creaked and the assorted city clamor carried me off.

I don't know how long I'd been out, only that when I awoke I was enshrouded in full darkness. My father still lived, probably having not yet risen a hair's suspicion over my absence. The mixture of grief and shame prohibited my rise. Sitting on the floor, I must have looked like a man after a fight lost outside a last-stop inn.

My eyes were adjusting to the black.

Peeking out from our blankets was a purse Somyellia had left behind.

An urge prompted that I crawl forward. Much to my hopes, I found inside this purse a small pouch of opium. I had partaken of it with her before. Small inhales here and there were enough to scramble the mind and titillate the senses, putting me in with sprites of the forest and pinprick demons that pranced and danced on and in me.

This time was to be different, though. On my hands and knees I crawled to a corner. I'd put together a bag in case some calamity required our egress; I had always imagined Somyellia, Celly, and I running off to some distant land, or maybe hacking a life out of a giving thicket somewhere deep in the magic-haunted wilderland. I sifted through loose silver, garments, candles, a corked vial, a loaf of bread which had molded horrendously, until at last I found what I'd been searching for: flint and steel.

With great care, I was able to burrow a hole in the side of the vial. With some additions found around the house, I built, as best I could, a vessel to billow my lungs.

A candle lit my back, facing the graves below, I commenced burning the remnants of my mistress's favored drug.

Once fully enveloped, I crawled to the edge of the collapsed wall and hovered over all the graves. Looking as if miles below, they glimmered with the glow of nearby street lamps and the few candles that burned in the land of the dead. Here, my soul was at zero.

I found what it was to possess utter rage. A rage that pulsated slowly and made all the world turn gray. I choked on dust and learned not to lament on the cliffs of lamentation. I remembered not to remember, and then the winds passed me. I ripped at my chest. I sat crouched, eyes staring into a ruined valley that I had never known. I gave myself to the gods of destruction, but they did not take me. I waited for my takers to claim me, but they did not come. No howling wind carrying my raiders from the shores of recallable time. No hordes of flesh and noise.

In what could have been ages later, Somyellia found me crouched in a damp corner on the bottom floor. The moldy loaf eaten, along with other things strewn about that neither of us could pinpoint by species or origin. I was naked, covered in dirt and parched with a horrible thirst. Even for a black-magic hooker from the Thunder Bustle, my ghoulish appearance stopped Somyellia in her high leather boots. Putting aside her carnal duties, with the care of a seasoned midwife, she nursed me back to health and to sanity. In a volley of screams and cradled flailing, I slowly began to let go of many things.

※ ※ ※

THE YEARS THAT FOLLOWED my running away were so full of chaos and poverty that only a morbid collage of memories remains. For all the swirling turmoil of abuse and neglect, I had been a boy who was well-fed, regularly schooled, and had ample means of washing off the residue of corpses and perspiration. All of that was gone.

I do recall the first few weeks as a vivid, sick sort of game. The Metropolitan Ward was summoned. Word found a way of trickling back to my ears that during their searches for me, many homes of former tutors and childhood friends whom I hadn't seen in years were ransacked as frustrations increased. My old laboratory had to eventually be discovered. I could too easily envision the laughing gaggle of mailed Wardsmen pilfering through it all.

As heavy hooves approached in brutish unison, I would scurry into the sewers or hide behind the wheel of a cart. With a crude sketch of me in hand, orphanages were scoured. I guess they thought a boy from Templeton would frighten after a night or two under the care of the Nilghorde streets. Little did they know me.

I was resolve, colder than rain on the mountain. I wasn't going back. Every time I eluded their patrols, it only bolstered my lost but freed heart.

Finally, after weeks of hide and seek, it all ended. The Prime Marshall had probably told Father in careful terms that I'd most likely been abducted and was already chained inside some galley far out at sea.

Other than a book I'd stowed and an armful of anatomy works procured from the rear door of an unaware bookstore, my youthful education had met its terminus. But this only, I'd told myself, was good reason to revisit my favorites. I read my third volume of *Poems of the Classics* so many times that its pages became frail with a sort of rot and rub. Reciting the voyage of Omiel the doomed Mariner and the poetry of Denom Vandahl were regular occurrences in my bleak obscurities.

For food, I started out by using all of my trapping skills. Hundreds of rats and several pigeons later, I took to joining those who haunted the crooked bricked jungle in search of money. If I wasn't able to find work—maybe a cheap laborer on some city project or sweeping the rubble left from all the statues being chiseled on Do-Gooder's Row—I learned through painful trial and error the grim arts of the street.

IV: The Caress

DESPITE THE BATTLES WITH food deprivation that came with having run away, I grew well in frame. Shoulders stretched outward. My chest grew slabs of beef. I had limbs of vein and sinew, and my lower legs were as thick as my upper arms. A boyish face melted away. By the time the Do-Gooder's Row statues looked like men trying to free their lower halves out of blocks of stone, my summer-field hair had taken to looking like that of my late mother's, both in its darkness and its length. I fit well with the orgy of maliciousness that populated the haunts of Nilghorde, which I'd come to call home.

On occasion, I resorted to desperate acts of violence. Eating a plate of cabbage and rabbit with bloody hands was barely a step above the beasts of the forest. I had at first pitied my victims, but soon savored the taste of bursting cooked flesh or boiled mushrooms in spite of the screams necessary to acquire it all.

One night this led me to a scuffle right next to where Somyellia and I's abandoned house met the graves.

The man squirmed, no more than an innkeeper who took the wrong turn. But this was the way of the world.

"Thirty silver—she just walked, from the mantel to the seating—I—my—" I had long ago picked up on the patterns in such pleas, all silenced with the butt of my knife.

The night now quiet, graveyard birds soon choired their calls. They seemed as if all around, though no matter how hard I tried, their perches remained hidden. As I gripped the fought-for purse, a hand caressed the back of my neck.

Every hair on my arms stood. I wheeled around to deliver a hard fate to the innkeeper's brave friend, the same grizzly fate for so many of the brave and misguided. But when I turned fully, I gazed at a sight even more peculiar: a slender man wrapped in shining black. There was no outstretched hand, for both of this stranger's were clapped together, no different than one of the many statues ornamenting the graves. The moon broke through the fog to radiate on his silk.

"Good evening," the man said.

By some nighttime trickery, I couldn't rise. For I surely tried, but all I could muster were a baffling series of slips, falls, and curses while the back of my neck burned and froze all at once.

"No need for such…barbarity," the man said, unclasping his hands and depriving me of my knife. The man straightened, looking at my blade, turning it this way and that. A milky light, brighter than the moon's clung to his cloak. "Do you always dispatch them?"

Odd, I know, but I felt whatever faculties had left me now making a slow return. The moment I was able, I rose to my feet and stood a clear head taller than this oddest of inquisitors. From this perspective, a far more familiar view, the stranger's regality lessened, and my knife in his grip looked more like a woman's hand fondling a Pelat machete.

"They call me Belot," the man said.

In my frenzy, better sense had escaped me. A few years around a woman like Somyellia had left me keen to know when black magic brewed. This man was a grave-walking necromancer. But threat of being turned into a toad wasn't my worry. In these queer years, dark practitioners were as liable to turn in lawbreakers at one of the many pavilions snapped together by confederacies made between the Ward and Ansul's True than sicking hexes on someone. Rumor had it that the cash reward could be handsome, especially if the misfit had violated both the laws of Man and Nature all at once. This stranger had seen my face, and though I'd only been caught violating the laws of Man, he—

"You don't speak?" he said.

"Bell-ought," I said, "split the purse and call it a night?"

"Do you always dispatch them?" he laughed, giving me back my knife. "Your holders of the *purse?*"

"No, never," I shot, jostling like I'd just discovered an itch, finishing with, "Well, not if they're smart about it." But this caused only more laughter. He looked over his shoulder at the abandoned house.

"Drab, rotted place. My own is but next door. Join me?" Before I could answer, he turned, taking no more than a step, "Bring him with us."

When I reached for the purse, I was ready for this bizarre courtship to come to an end. After all, that's what this Belot was after, for nobody disliked money. But this stranger responded to my grabbing in way that was uncharacteristic of a robber. He smiled. A smile that if placed on every man at once would put merchant's like Somyellia out of business. I hoisted the innkeeper on my shoulder and followed.

❋❋❋

"So YOU ARE THE source of all that noise." Mr. Belot gestured toward Somyellia and I's house. "Thought I'd have to call upon the zoo so they could retrieve some tenants on the lam. Spirited girl." I had to put down my second glass to laugh bashfully and spill wine.

It turned out Mr. Belot shared both my old tutor's nihilism and my fondness for capitalizing on the deceased. Mr. Belot's eyes glowed, followed by full admission that he was nothing short of astonished; how a "large knifeman from the streets" could know every bone in the human body. Mr. Belot's interest in my ambitions had swept away the initial discomfort I'd felt. Soon we were gabbing like drunken military wives.

As the night stretched, I ogled at the skulls and bones and books. The prowess of scales and cauldrons were unlike anything I'd ever seen, and it filled me with a bizarre joy that Mr. Belot's collection of femurs was larger than the one I'd amassed in the old cellar. Then there was the wooden table. On it were leather straps, pulled and worn taut. At Mr. Belot's request, I had lifted the moaning innkeeper onto it, during which I saw bloodstains that had seeped deep into the wood. My timid inquiry into this man's looming fate was met with Belot's caress. I don't recall what his answer was, only that I was sated. It was as if I'd been charmed, though a necromancer practicing such things was pure and utter silliness.

A second bottle of Grest opened talks about more pressing matters. To Mr. Belot, I would learn, the world was becoming harder for lovers of the dark and the courageous. "You see those silly statues, Seasmil?" he said. "Placating the masses; scared of their own shadows as good as a plague. Do-Gooder's Row is halfway built and Maecidion the Virulent is dying."

It was true, I supposed, at least to a degree. I'd seen the Chapwyn fliers swell in numbers and the pitchfork wielders soon follow. Although the poor and wretched had swollen even greater, a formidable army of limpers and squabbling hags, oaths to eradicate the world of wickedness seemed all that was necessary to satisfy the barking mob. But to people like me, such social ebb and flow meant about as much as what Lotgard shit last and where. I didn't want to tell Mr. Belot that those whose entire cosmos is the calling cookpot and alley didn't concern themselves with such prattle, especially dying royalty. But even I drank from the trickling stream of gossip—Maecidion, that lauded patriarch of Somyellia's, had indeed fallen ill.

Mr. Belot looked over the rim of his glass, "Times are changing, my hulking friend."

I am no hero, nor am I the stuff of legend. No kraken to best. No dragon to slay. My war was painfully simple. I had to survive, and even amidst the brawls and illness and thievery, I still clung to the hope of one day being, yes, a doctor. It was perhaps my greatest fortune then that Mr. Belot and I's interests shared a common component: bodies.

I left with a friend, a mentor, and most important of all, an employer. By the time Maecidion died, I was leading a pack of rogues. I would put intimidation to even better use, but Mr. Belot's thoughts on confrontation were even more prudent than my own. Most of the time, I would be working alone, and, at Mr. Belot's direction, digging up graves.

V: Seasmil and Snier

A
ND WHAT ARE YOU fine gentlemen gabbing on about?" Somyellia larked, appearing at the base of our stoop with groceries. "How Maecidion is still rumored to rise again, even after these six long years we've been without him," her hair thrown back by the wind, "or how that immortal monument to stupidity over in Do-Gooder's is finally showing its figures below their knees?"

"Snier here," I replied, not done taunting my colleague, "*studied math*. Below the knees is, that's over eighty percent done. Right, Snier?"

"Oh, we're just talking about the time you tried to sneak him into your old place," Tymothus Snier said from the top step as I bounced up to lend Somyellia a hand.

"That one," she said, handing me the basket. "Seasmil tell you how—"

"How the fiendish guards persuaded me to find shelter elsewhere," I said, "yeah yeah."

"Well," said Snier, who had a fashion for clasping his hands together more girlish than any third Somyellia'd ever brought into our bed. "And shelter elsewhere you lovebirds did. Shall we?"

We all went inside, where, as per usual, Snier began his prattle about our "menagerie of skulls" and the "religious graffiti." My contributions, at least, were gradual preparations for the Institute, but even I had to concede how Somyellia's flare for gratuitous macabre had taken over our decorative tastes. But, though he was reluctant to admit it, our decorations were becoming as neighborly to Snier as we who owned them.

"Glad you'll suffer the market for us, baby," I said, tasked with a plum jar that Somyellia'd handed me. "They'd just come up with some new rule, say I violated it," the reluctant lid opened and spun, "and jail my ass."

Snier was quick to agree. "You are worse than what they got in the dungeon downtown," he said. "Sommy, let me tell you, having bumped into your menacing hunk here—while working his trade, no less—hell, I would have called the Ward. Bite marks, scars, clothing of nothing but black and questionable greens—well, let's just say that raven hair of yours, Seasmil, doesn't always look as charming."

I saw that the effeminate thief wasn't the only one looking me up and down. Work had taken Somyellia on the road for almost a week. I watched as she fondled our bone wind chimes.

Like most domiciles on the Avenue of Red Wolf, our place was coffin-like and smelled sour from an unfindable leak in the sewer pipes.

For me though, it was perfect. Although fewer than in my teen years, my dissections hadn't stopped. I'd made a pact with myself that I'd proudly kept: I never once took a human life in order to collect my materials. I came perilously close once, but two of my cohorts beat me to it. Their lust for inflicting pain and their general bristling nature, I had opted to view in quiet disdain, but that night I was grateful. Our assignment had tried to rise from his bed to cast some hex on us, and by the looks of his gaunt and soulless slaves, he was far too dangerous to be shown mercy. I'd left that night with one of his slave's arms tucked into my belt. Her limb had been meant to serve as a premiere piece to cut open and inspect, but its ceaseless twitching forced me to give up and throw it away.

This rule that I'd self-imposed may have been more difficult to honor if I hadn't been a grave robber. When taking my work home with me made a stack too high, our tiny but high-walled backyard took care of the surplus. Like jagged teeth, towering slums hung over our yard, appearing in opium-induced stirs as looming onlookers. In the queer hours of morning, I would bury all that was to be buried. Snier, like a good neighbor, admitted once that it lullabied him, the soft digs of the shovel.

The three of us reclaimed our stoop and I packed the pipe. The steps were still warm, but it would be night soon. Somyellia sidled onto my lap. It was easy to forget how fiercely she'd blossomed into full womanhood when she gave me her girlish smile. My gratitude had remained two-fold. This beauty wasn't just cause for erections all over Nilghorde, but because of her beauty our rent was still usually paid.

"The witch's bosom still gives milk, Snier." The cloud of smoke that burst from my mouth ate Somyellia like a wedding veil.

"Yeah," Snier said, sounding like he was already mulling over our night's work. "Pass it here so I can share such enlightenments."

One puff was all it ever took for Snier; not hard to imagine, being that he wasn't much bigger than one of my legs. The smoke tickled his lungs, then his brain, then shot out those blue eyes onto the beautiful filth of Nilghorde.

"How'd I get here," Snier said, "Nilghorde—*ugh*." He had a habit of doing this. We'd usually sit and watch. I'd gape. Somyellia'd usually giggle. "Not sure where to start," he went on, "that's all. Too hard on yourself. Always have been. You abandoned the thought of it. Besides, looks fade—like your hairline. Too hard on yourself. Always have been. Robbery is—"

"Snier," Somyellia said, "kind sir, may we have our pipe back now?"

"Robbery is too dangerous. Street-thieving too competitive. Besides—here you go, Sommy—the margins are too low." Snier was still carrying on as we made our way back into our side of the duplex. "Oh well, every now and again we get a good load."

"We sure do," Somyellia said, grabbing my thickened member and shutting our door with her heel.

Draped in a fresh intestinal track, Somyellia ground on top of me. Once spent, our pipe returned, cradled in her hands, the golden snake. Too stunned to go at it again, exalted visions came to me in patches, like a dreary giant who was blinking as he lumbered across the world.

"...You will be a doctor," I heard, coming to. My love was on her side, reading my latest batch of notes and sketches, bare, save the scrolls ribboned over her thigh. "We'll have droves of bodies to spin our wealth."

When I came to again, Somyellia was on the floor, dreamily covering our floorboards in the symbols of her craft with her red and white paints.

"I can buy a batch of girl slaves," Somyellia said, "and have a row of wiggling rumps waiting for you after a long day of curing washerwomen of their cough. Our garden will explode with all the illegal vines and bulbs. Finer arts demand it, you know. Many coffins will have to be dumped out for some of the advanced stuff. And I'll need close to constant petting too." I went for my work tools lying next to a jar of thumbs, a sight that would have made our landlord's head pop off if he ever gulped down the courage to come in. "But if my brute is too busy writing books and cutting out tumors," she blew me a kiss as I waved her off amiably, "then the boy slaves will just have to do."

⁂

"SHE REALLY THINKS I can get into the—"

"Institute of Human Sciences, never heard of it," Snier said, rearranging the picks in his work-belt.

Copping to the sarcasm: "Just need the tuition."

We skirted a culvert and waded through a sliver of marsh. The night had come swiftly as I'd snored and drooled. During which, Snier reminded me, he'd paced all over our stoop until at last I emerged with our crowbar and short-handled shovels. My tools, of course, were now tucked away in my bag.

But the moon and stars this night were remarkably shy. Hiding our larger tools was probably as unnecessary as scaling the roots of an old oak to make our way through a hole in the cemetery fence.

Snier and I had met on a similar night. When Snier had fled to Nilghorde, his better judgment swayed him to put the sex trade on sabbatical. Snier had said his suspicions were confirmed when it trickled down that the Ward had ransacked every boy brothel. In fact, he'd told me a whole lot, which as we slinked past the first of several guardhouses, my amused mind replayed his grandest story yet:

Without a coin in his purse, Snier had said, one evening he'd sat and watched as a funeral procession went by. The clamor had been clad in jewels. Gold plates weren't sealed in some vault, but being banged by a parade of mourners.

Breaking into mausoleums was easy enough for a competent thief, and Snier surely was. But too many were in parts where antsy, spear-kneading watchmen marched about. Though it never ceased to make his skin crawl, the safer bet was the endless sea of graves.

Some graves are forgotten as soon as they are lowered, not even a shovel's load covers some of the more extreme cases. Others are in the outskirts of any given cemetery, usually the side where overgrowth seems bent on reclaiming the land for the wild.

One night, Snier wanted to try his luck in the Maedraderium. To him, as to most of us, the Maedraderium was a small city of twinkling lavish homes for those far beyond the ability to appreciate it all. Hoping to wash himself and bicker to no one about the heaviness of the coffin he'd given up on, he said he'd followed the gurgling of a nearby fountain. He went around one mausoleum wall just to slam face-first into another—his words. He wondered how a wall could have felt so warm on such a cool night. Then an arm pinned him flat to the ground.

His kicks pitter-pattered against not a wall, but a man's chest. Snier said his dagger was smacked away like a troublesome nat. Screaming may have alerted an eager watchman. Prison seemed like a dream by comparison, but his mouth was sealed shut by the man's large hand.

It was broken at the tip, but a thick knife flashed in caught starlight. As the knife rose higher, maybe it was his lust for beauty that pulled Snier to see the ornate casket behind the man on top of him. Yes, behind this man, this unrepenting fiend, a casket sat pulled out of the earth, and it sat unopened.

"Ikin owen it," Snier said against the palm covering his mouth, his eyes clinched like dungeon vises. After a moment Snier felt the hand lift off. "I can open it."

I let him up. The locks on that damn thing had cost me the tip of my knife, but with a little tooling, Tymothus Snier opened the griffin-emblazoned casket with a final *chunk*.

A year later, Snier finally believed me when I'd said that I had no plans on killing him that night, that and he had long since moved into the other half of our duplex. Alliances weren't just for the Ward and royal Houses. Nothing better than combining some muscle with a little coy lock work.

"Snier," I said, back in the present and entering a thicket of headstones, "remember the coffin that had that gold dildo inside?"

Good ol' Sniery had seen such things before—in fact, he may have been the only person in all Mulgara to have encountered one in two different professions.

"Can we just get to it?"

We laid our tools on the grass, but I whipped out the opium.

"Yeah," Snier soon giggled, "I sold it to a Chapwyn priest." Any watchman or fellow grave robber may have run screaming from our ghouls-feeding laughter. "Should have given it to Somyellia...sorry, no offense."

"Meh," I said, disenthralling myself from a comfortable headstone, "just her job. You wouldn't understand." Snier's stare tickled me. "Now *that* was just a joke, little buddy. Let's get to work." I grabbed a shovel and got digging.

"We need to split the spoils the way you said you used to." Snier said. We'd hit a good one! A bloated noble stuffed in a coffin studded in bronze-lined jade. "And to think, he thought going the *in the ground* route would fool entrepreneurs like us, Mr. Oleugsby."

"Ansul's ass!" I let out. Quieting myself, I leaned in to stare at the plates and goblets. Disgracing the Chapwyn church father's name had just been upped from time in the pillory to a lopped-off head, and grave robbing had been a death sentence for years—whether at the executioner's axe or ripped limb from limb by the offended and turned loose meek. Being killed twice over was a distilling notion, but the smiles on both our dirty faces gleamed still. I said without taking my eyes of our treasure, "The old arrangement was I'd keep the jewelry; he just wanted the body." I glanced over. Snier appeared to be listening, though steadfastly working a jeweled bracer off a leathery arm. "Still want it how I used to do it?"

"There," Snier exhaled. "Got her—I thought you were the one who only wanted the body?"

"No. It's a great way to collect material, sure," I explained. Snier handed me up the loot. Soft *tinks* and *tanks* sang as our bag swelled.

"Materials is mostly why I do it now. That and bills. By the time I got back in business, I could hardly afford a bread crumb. But, such is your fate when a squadron of Ansul's True catches you slipping rings off lower clergy."

Snier chuckled while handing up a goblet. "That story made it all the way to Pelliul."

"You're kidding? Yeah, I'd probably have enough money for tuition by now if it weren't for that storm of torches and hymns. But, yeah, back when Mr. Belot hired me, it was simple: More bodies for him, more coin from him. I kept anything I found—which was usually nothing but worm shit—and he got first crack at the haul."

Jumping out of the hole, "And for that there was a wage?"

"And a decent one," jumping down to cut off noble ears. "Of course, there was more to it."

"Not sure I want to know," Snier said.

"It's a shame Belot's gone. Probably dead."

"Seaz, I got to finally ask it. What the hell does taking apart a few stiffs over and over have anything to do with becoming a doctor? Why not—"

—We were on their bellies. Out from nowhere a clamor of mounted watchmen had appeared. One said "Opium smell," thankfully riding right past us and then disappearing.

We slithered all the way back to the oak.

Once on the streets my heart pounded less erratically. I continued, "For practice. So, yeah, I worked for him about a year, then he just vanished like he went up in smoke. Metaphorically apt too, I found signs there'd been a fire where he usually worked. Somyellia thinks Belot disappeared because this one vile man he had me take care of may have had even viler friends."

"Fires. Vile friends. Somyellia hasn't pieced it all together? She's from folk not too far off from your Mr. Belot."

"Only folk of hers I've ever met is that onion-headed cousin, Irion. Always tasking her out with brews and broths. I ask her what for and she just clams up and tells me *family business*."

#

WE MADE IT HOME and divided the spoil, as we always did. No fuss. No squabble. The haul put food in the gullet, but greater things called. Not long after, Snier broke the news to me that he'd had his fill of grave dirt. I'd made a friend. I'd cared for the little thief from Pelliul, but as is my fate, like Belot, he too would vanish.

VI: The Pauper Morgue

I AM SEASMIL, AND Death has followed me from an early age. Mother and Celly had left the world in different ways, but stalked my dreams equally. Death was as a part of life to me as was ink to a book. So when I found Somyellia dead on our floor I didn't scream. Life owes us nothing.

She had died suddenly, without warning, at the hand of a ruthless venereal disease. Carried coolly by men but cursing the innards of females, I knew this from the blood that had let from all her orifices and pooled over the symbols she'd repainted. Although I had to be a carrier, she was most likely infected while working her trade.

In this moment she was terribly beautiful, her nose and mouth spilling forth blood as wicked as her ancestors that danced under the winter moon. Those golden eyes stared at me as if to ask one final question. Her skin was still warm under the robe she sometimes wore when practicing her finer craft.

I lifted her off the floor. Her head hung far back and her hair waggled in her blood, like the fine tip of a large paintbrush. Hugging her was all one could do. Silence. I had never been in a place so quiet, not even the old cellar or the furthermost grave.

My own blood roared. I told myself she'd gone back to revel with her kind; wrought not of our world. And though this made me feel no better, after a moment the silence seemed broken by echoes from some far off place, a place I partly understood her to be. All of this could have been my own wishful thinking, of course; maybe the worms were the last to taste my sweet Somyellia.

I laid her on her side of the bed and went through her satchel. After, I went through our drawers and chests.

With a handful of silver, I laid beside her. She'd never once spoken about her burial wishes, an amazing feat considering the nature of our usual talks. She may have wanted a spiraling funeral pyre, an obsidian mausoleum, to be hacked to bits and fed to the night creatures she loved so dearly.

I kept her for days. Telling myself I was waiting on Irion worked for a little while. He was, after all, the only family member she'd ever introduced me to, and proper burial was I figured a family affair. But he never came, and as a day or two passed that reasoning melted away. Not being able to say goodbye stood firmly in its place.

To clean her meant moving her to the kitchen table. I walked around her studiously, solemnly; death had managed to steal many of the features we are so accustomed to.

An urge entered me as I circled the table. Pulling apart her legs, now heavy and cold, I positioned myself. In all the sexual voyages between us, all the desecration of graves, and juices spent, I'd never done this. How could I? She had on occasion teased me of my appetite, and joked I was capable of such "selfish indulgences."

As usual, she was right. I entered a place that was always so inviting and warm, now a rough tunnel. In the midst of my efforts I heard grunting. I believed for just a moment that I had thrusted her back to life. It was I who grunted, and the moment's realization came right as I did.

I wrapped her in a sheet and prepared to enter the streets. Much coaxing and the coins I'd scrounged up days earlier got me a mule to carry Somyellia to the Pauper Morgue.

Taking her to a place designated for the nameless and faceless forgotten made me ill to the core. Hooded, in midday, I took the laden mule down Red Wolf, over the little white bridges that ran through Nilghorde Commerce, past the Tower of the Waning Moon, and finally through winding roads that made the strange district called the The Dead Kettle.

Arriving at the front offices of the morgue, I tethered the mule and stared up at the fat man's nearby tower we'd once raided. Since then it had withered terribly, as if the ultimate perversions once contained within had howled free, leaving the rook beaten by decay beyond the normal brutality of the sun and rain.

I carried Somyellia through the doors of the Pauper Morgue. The transaction was as brief as one would expect. Then a pair of pale bald men took her.

Looking at these two, if you saw them you would find them disgusting and queer, and not be ashamed of it. Stubby legs supported flab up to the neck, and pouty bottom lips held spittle ready to drip. It was too easy to see the types of men that had paid Somyellia over the years. Just as easily, to see them mongering over her body the moment my back was turned. Eventually letting go of my knife's handle, I helped them unwrap her from the sheet.

"What do you want on the tombstone?" the shorter one asked.

Throughout the years, I have read dozens of excerpts in poems and books, the ones loaded with saccharine romancing, and I wished I'd used a number of them. Particularly striking was a line out of *Songs in Regal Twilight*, authored by Vandahl five hundred years before I was born. At the time, though, all I could do was fight back a surge of tears and scribble out what was clawing:

SOMYELLIA ORDRID

CAPTOR OF MANY HEARTS, RULER OF ONE

A Black Lamb In Your Arms Do I Hope To Find You

"Good sir," the taller one said, sounding a degree more elegant than his counterpart and pulling me back to the world. "We are looking to replace an employee…very soon. The position requires the ability to read and write."

"Skills elusive to many willin' to work here," the short one said.

"We don't mean to ask you this without regard to the tragedies that befell you," the tall one said, brushing a hand over Somyellia, "but we need a strong back most urgently."

I don't know if I had death written on my face. Maybe these little trolls, so close to it on a daily basis, were able to see things others couldn t. This opportunity seemed to fall out of the sky and onto the lap of a man well-adjusted to life's apathy. This was so harmoniously ideal that my shift to excitement with the smell of Somyellia still on my skin pelted me with guilt.

Who was she really, though? Mocking her by remembering the version that suited me best held no love or honor. She was strong in life, and surely would laugh hideously at my weakened state. She would have nodded with that haunting nod, then "Do it, lover." Whereever she was, she had no need for my indecision.

Yes, this is how I got here.

Telling them I accepted made them smile—sluggy, melted smiles—and when they told me the wages I almost danced on the ceiling. I wasn't going to rival the vaults of the ruling, but by my quick arithmetic, in a year I would be able to enroll at the Institute.

The former mortician was gone in no time. The first few days were shadowing the two waddling managers. My workspace was the morgue itself, vast and set back from the street. Inside, its walls made a stone honeycomb that contained bodies in all sizes and conditions. At its center, where I'd spend most of my time, was the table.

Above my station, the domed ceiling was a cap of painted glass. Hilarious in its irony, it depicted the poor and pious being whisked away by serene carriers to some orange and golden field. Waiting for them, Tersiona sat in a throne of wheat, surrounded by Ansul and a ring of lesser figures. By day, the ceiling provided a glowing vale of sunlight, and on the nights I chose not to go home, church icons holding books and teapots glared down on my solitude.

Following a downhill path, my designated cart was to be led to an iron door on the northern edge of the cemetery, an edge well known to me. This door was much like a cellar hatch, bolted on a granite frame leading to the Pauper Vault. The dead poor were dropped to reside forever with carrion, foulness, and things that scampered from the light. Even for me, the stench that belched up from that darkness didn't only offend the nostrils, but clawed at the skin and smothered.

Continuing downhill were the graves for those buried with just enough money to avoid the filling pit. And there was Somyellia.

At the end of my first day, I went down to see her. I sat at her graveside and stared across the sea of weathered stone teeth. Across the vast distance, through the gleaming spires of Laugher's Lot, I could make out our abandoned house, a speck that was once our grandest meeting place.

Pain exposes itself when it chooses to, and as most harden with the passing years it becomes an indistinguishable part of life. I leaned against her brand new stone and wept. It's like Vandahl wrote: *"Life is but wild flowers in the graveyard."*

A void in me was undeniably ripped open after Somyellia left. Perhaps that is why I fell into my work so. I enjoyed the sweating from the lifting, all legal for the first time.

It became a routine: inspect the day's load, tend the horse assigned to the morgue, attach her to the cart, throw a body on the table, report, hoist it into said cart, repeat. The short report was more gratifying than any bundle of obscure notes I'd made on my own. Cause of death—best guess sufficed, physical description, name (if known), a few other details, and then on to the next.

My bosses, I came to find out, were Qells; a once magnificent house that had long rotted away from lordship. They were pleased by my performance. So much so, in fact, that after only a month they never stepped foot in the morgue again. Their time was better spent in the front office, delving into the keepsakes of freshly brought bodies, dealings with cutthroats, and occasionally supporting the coup of some ambitious rising figure.

Though Snier and Somyellia were gone, I remained in my studio, or I should say my possessions did. The Pauper Morgue became my real home—as the commoners who pass out bread rather than the blade say, "It's where the heart lies." Sleeping on a mat of blankets in a favored corner, book in hand, and well-fed from lamplight was my only joy. Street murmurs crawled back to me that, not long after taking employment, an attentive group of urchins took me for evicted or dead. I laugh at the thought of them burgling only to run headlong into my ferine collections.

Some bodies at the morgue needed dissection to root out cause of death. In no time, I bore witness to the many malfunctions of our vulnerable flesh. Diseases that attached to organs, fiercely and without remorse, always made me miss her something awful.

The few bodies that were to accompany tombstones I'd separate early. Piling them like a stack of fingered and footed firewood reminded me a lot of Belot's place. Once filled, the cart would go to the mass grave and I'd play the game of trying to drop them in ways that would achieve the greatest cracks and thuds. Most memorable,

I once invoked a peculiar squeal, after which I softly closed the door and backed away.

My bosses relished the tight-lipped approach. I was met with freedom, more coin, and ample food. My predecessor, I imagined, must have expressed some grievance with their dealings, and I wondered what hill of bones in that subterranean pit he occupied.

In time, I surmised they thought I killed Somyellia. In addition to being tolerant of murder, with my literary skills and build, they figured me the perfect subordinate. I never confirmed this, but a mind educated by both the works of scholars and the streets possesses the ability to cut through clout and inanities like a robber's knife.

Much like a child enamored in summer, I lost track of time. Weeks became months, and those too seemed to fly by with the wave of dead that gave me my livelihood.

You would have thought Nilghorde would have been desolate in a mere season. No matter the ebb and flow, the city remained as bustling and lively as ever. The occasional stroll to my studio would take me up Red Wolf, examining the living with new eyes. "I wonder when I'll be seeing you?" I'd sometimes say, a couple of times too loud.

My so-called experiments ceased entirely. Dreams of becoming a doctor were barely an afterthought. A bill on a dusty shelf.

Though dead, Somyellia had not left my heart nor my habits. Nights I would wake to see her gliding from a darkened corner of the morgue. It ended as soon as my mind took the step out of the world of dream and into the forever disappointing world we temporarily occupy. It exposed life's pallid and stagnant nature, a few punishing seasons of hot and cold. These visions were only a phase, possibly due to another phase of mine, one in which a young womanly corpse would be examined for far too long, though never treated to the carnal activities that had closed my one and only love.

My existence had met a livable rhythm. I'd never expected, or wanted, the sun-soaked slogging of many who claim to live the good life. I knew from an early age I was meant to dwell in other passions. I had money for the few things that interested me. I fought a small war with opium and won, resulting in an additional layer of meat on my hide. I read endlessly, making sure to visit libraries and vendors of the book and scroll. The dead had befriended me, and while sitting among the morgue's more comfortable nooks I often fell asleep leaned against their silent company.

VII: The Ritual

O N THE ANNIVERSARY OF Somyellia's death, I abandoned my
duties to sit beside her grave. The bouquet of roses and lilies
I had laid were for the day. The wreath of coiled orphedilias, for the
coming night.

Staring at her stone, some lettered grooves had been corrupted
by a year's mold. As I scraped the mold with my fingernails,
I remembered. It's funny how the bereaved mind rushes back to the
last time we've seen the dead when they were not. I was certainly
no exception.

❀❀❀

ALL MALEVOLENT MASQUERADE WAS always our favorite holiday.
She'd told me the party at the Rogaire mansion had gone off
without a hitch, but I was still sour that I had to spend the night
elsewhere. Duty came first, she'd said, but she'd also mused how she
too would have much rather joined me on the one night a year the
proper spilled into graveyards and disreputable bars, banging drums,
running up tabs, puking on headstones, and cutting up roasted pigs
while dressed as goblins and muskrats.

Somyellia lay in bed with her eyes shut. Some nighttime clamor
out on Red Wolf had distracted her, but she'd resumed one of

her fonder pastimes. She dug her hand through the jar of severed tongues. Pulling a shriveled one out and giving it a good lick, "Thee neighborly would be less incorrigible if it weren't for those drat newcomers, by rights," said Somyellia. One more, swollen and still holding its redness, proved to be decidedly male. "Not that bonnet, woman! Makes you look a frumpish bar trout," she boomed, and then her voice returned to normal. "Lovely stuff."

I stood there, drying my hair. "So we're going to be swimming in silver soon for all this?"

"More to life than metal," lidding the jar, "one as keen for stomach tubes and finger bones as you knows this," Somyellia said. "Don't sound too Chapwyn on me." I tossed a severed hand that we used for intimate petting off the bed and flopped down beside her. "Mediocre in the many ways that he may be," Somyellia continued, "Irion easily dominated the Rogaire prison master. *Asking for a guard change and an escort out of that lovely dungeon* was no harder than robbing graves in a blind man's graveyard with a silent shovel."

As she came up on her hands and knees, the window above our bed held the night. She studied the angle of the moon. I studied the sleek dip of her back and bare buttocks. "It's almost time," she said, staying me and hopping toward her wardrobe.

"It's a wonder that termite-eaten box doesn't explode," I said. Rummaging through the clutter, she swung out ribbons of dazzling green before tossing it in the trash.

"Sexy lizard costume?" I snickered.

"Ansul's ass, don't make me relive it."

"I still don't get it."

"Told you, my beast, I introduced Irion and Morlia years ago."

"Eight years."

"You *do* listen. And soon, as you know, after they'd met they agreed Morlia'd approach that dim prison master. Who knows, it could have been my tasking if Morlia hadn't been so insistent," giving the rummage a rest, her eyes sparkled, "but, of course, I would have tactfully explained I was already so uncompromisingly taken. But I knew it would work well. The weak charm Irion drenched her in probably wasn't even needed."

"Seduce the warden?"

"She is perfect for the prison master. Well," erupting in the laugh people do when ruminating on a joke's punch line, "perfect for both of them. Irion has really taken a liking to her."

This Morlia, the object of Irion's affection, had been Somyellia and I's third-lover many times in the earlier days. She'd stiffened me the first night I'd met the two of them as a teen in Templeton. Though I may have been overestimating Somyellia's sensitivity, I kept to myself my understanding of why men were so wrapped around Morlia's finger.

"The charm spell wasn't necessary," I said, trying to make it sound like a question.

"Hadn't seen Cousin Irion in ages," Somyellia said, perhaps wanting to shift the course of our conversation, "since playing in our family's gardens as children. Then there he is, rapping at the doors. Right after Maecidion died, actually. Funny how a death in the family can change people. Irion acted quite differently, the way he moved and even how he spoke. A lot like Maecidion used to, in fact."

"That's fantastic—so listen, if he's so low in your branches or what have you, why the servant-girl role whenever he graces our stoop?"

"When you talk like that sometimes it makes me think I really should have entertained Morfil's advances," she said, successfully irritating me. I watched her as she pulled out what she'd been looking for: her dark robe covered in family regalia. She wore it only when practicing the type of witchcraft that demanded her utmost.

It didn't take living with a witch to know her work was outlawed. Along with the parchment plague of new maxims about labor class virtue nailed everywhere, many false witches had been rounded up in plazas and burned to kick off the Years of Peace. Now all that remained seemed to be the real ones. Although there were those practicing black magic who stalked the periphery, Somyellia's House had, according to her, earned the trust of the evil gods. Such trust bestowed on the Ordrids the secrets of their trickery. But it came with a heavy price. When her family called, she said she had to listen. Noticing I was still waiting for an answer, she only said, "Tersiona weeps for a reason."

"I'll remember that. Who penned that lofty explanation for all life's quandaries, you or Vandahl?"

"We've been over this," she sighed. Somyellia knew I didn't care for Irion. He lived somewhere in the Bustle, so it was rare he appeared at our door. But even during such rarities, I always found a reason to slink on over to Snier's side.

"It's just I hear so many times," I said, launching my impersonation of her that made her blood boil, "*my beast—my beast, I can't do this or that or that and this*—but then he shows up and your schedule's wide open."

"Seasmil."

"Wide open."

"Seasmil," she said, culling a tone that started to bring me down out of webs in the rafters.

"Wide open as...like the Moliahenna River's mouth after a damn flood."

"Vandahl pen that?" she said, returning to bed.

✻✻✻

"I'LL LET YOU GET to witchery then," I said after we'd finished, climbing off of her. Irion's most recent visit was to ask of Somyellia her major discipline. And she'd done her part. Somyellia had touched some warden who Morlia had somehow found a way to send barreling over to her. The curse had been locked by waves of her hand that she told me was passed off as nothing more than churlish girl anger.

Somyellia was happy to help. The House of Rogaire had wronged the House of Ordrid, and Irion—in this newfound severity Somyellia occasionally mentioned—was just tidying up family business.

Even the common-most dung-scooper on the common-most street knew that when the Conqueror's campaign had swept over the peninsula, ending at the doorsteps of Maecidion's keep, deals were struck and the land was renamed.

Yet after enough talks from the bottom of our pillows, I myself could orate the finer points in her family's spiderweb of shifting powers and trickery.

The tale told within Ordrid confines was that after necromancy had been outlawed, and Maecidion and his kind were allowed to practice in secret, it didn't take long for the freshly outfitted Metropolitan Ward, and the people cheering them, to look for a new threat to their newfound tranquility. Rinmauld Rogaire, father of the warden they all hated, was one of the chief legislators after the Conqueror turned to his unyielding seclusion. It turns out that law was the one magic blacker than necromancy. Extorting Maecidion had been both legal and lucrative. Keeping the House of Ordrid's share of agreed-upon war spoils was payment for Rinmauld not sicking on Somyellia and Maecidion's House the society that had as soon forgotten war as was quick to start a new one.

An Ordrid vendetta on the House of Rogaire had been talked about in dark circles for decades. For reasons not entirely explained, her cousin Irion had picked up the proverbial hatchet on behalf of the late Maecidion, and now apparently planned on burying it into the heads of the Rogaires who remained.

Somyellia now had to conduct the final ritual and erupt the curse they'd set. I personally didn't bother much with her duties in this arena, but I also hadn't really in her leg-spreading one either. Our time together was all that mattered; however, even I had learned that all "great curses" required three parts. The victim must be touched by the curser or cursers, and she and Irion had both done that at different times. The curser or cursers must lock in their work with particular gestures, as she had done at the party. Now, the final act was to be executed. It would take time and the moon at the right position.

She began her work as I grabbed my shovel and crowbar to head out to do mine.

VIII: Warhorse on the Horizon

P URPOSE TENDS TO BE a cruel morning, waking you suddenly and thoroughly. My dour harmony, my focused aloneness, was to be disrupted once more, and once more it would come out of nowhere, as is its preference.

One day, we had a delivery. A giant man, killed by some disease, lay on my table bloated and blue. Normally I would have commenced to working, and the larger than normal corpse would have been in the cart and ready for transport.

But I walked around the table in the same fashion that I had done with Somyellia back on Red Wolf. This cold mound looked familiar, causing me without effort to mumble near-forgotten words.

Tension filled the room, making home the places saved for the cobwebs and rodents grown fat on my occasional forgetting to close the back door.

I knew who this reminded me of, with deathly certainty. I hadn't thought about him in ages, and he had been as dead to me as the inhabitants of the mass grave.

For a moment I wondered if it was him. But I was looking down on flabby jowls on top of a weak chin. His hair had been the same color, but coarse and curled. Just to be sure, and with some effort, I rolled the corpse onto his side. No, no giant scar on his back.

I had completely forgotten about it until using it as an identifier. My father had a deep swathe between his shoulders from a battle in the first campaign he'd ever embarked on.

He'd told of the ambushing Pelats and their crude, bony weapons. How they had skewered his horse and overwhelmed him. How he had one pinned to the ground, and how a moment before the fatal strike a sneaky Pelats opened up his back in the vain attempt to save his fellow savage.

Surviving the ordeal with a fresh trophy of tongues and charms, a field hospital repaired Father's back, and adorning citations followed in his recovery.

It may have been the thick neck, or some indescribable similarity, but I couldn't shake what I began to feel. An idea germinated in me, powerful and driven. Closure, something I had never known. It began to squeak and plea from the core of my being.

The rest of the day was spent in a hurried discontent.

After days of research in a back room at the Nilghorde Hall of Records, I learned that he was indeed still alive. He must have had squandered his war spoils. The house in Templeton had been sold long ago. Shoeing for a Ward substation, and likely led with a rabid taste for Black Monk, he took up residence in a small loft off Iron Belfry Boulevard. There, most roads and weaving allies remained nameless, and the view cast on a once thriving populace that hadn't progressed in the better part of a century.

When I took my covert observations on foot, for a fleeting moment I saw, silhouetted by firelight, a large figure limp past a window. Cloaked in a black hood, I moved like a rat. The few Metropolitan Ward who trotted by were oblivious. But I wanted to be sure my efforts would not be thwarted. I needed perfect concealment, and a moonless night was soon to arrive.

Then it came. Midafternoon in my mortician's cart, after a brief stop inside a blacksmith's, my horse and I rested under the massive Gahlerrion Bridge. Flowing under the bridge was the Moliahenna, or *Black Tongue*, cutting deep and swift through the heart of Nilghorde and spilling into the sea. At its shores, parked under an abutment, I watched the sunset and scowled at approaching beggars.

After the sun had completely died and the cold winds began, I reentered the streets. The clopping of the hooves and random squeaks of cart wheels echoed against the bricks of homes and shops. For some reason they all sounded too loud. Irksomely loud even. The glare of a Wardsmen and sideways glances from passing carriages sunk me in my seat. Eventually I passed under the Do-Gooder's Row statues, and began ascending narrow cobblestone.

If there had been a moon, around when it would have been at its zenith I crept the cart into the correct alley and cached it behind a withered hedge.

Hugging the veranda wall and unsheathing my knife, the time had come.

I was no Snier, but the poor man's lock before me was no match for the blade that wormed its way between iron and wood. When I felt the click and pressure release, I opened the door, painfully slow.

From what I had gathered, the bed was upstairs, and in his aged state it was reasonable to wager he'd be asleep. Although moonless, and candles out, I could see quite well. Maybe years spent in dark cellars or matching places had rendered me a brother to the night or the creatures therein. I was staring at a familiar parlor, though it felt a lifetime ago.

To my immediate right was the fanning display of sabers. Next to them, medals from the Far East, Pelat, and the massacres of Serabandantilith. To my left was a table in front of the very leather furnishings I'd once spilt milk on. My eyes passed closed doors to strain the exact shapes of stairs.

The distance between the front door and this stairwell was soon over taken. The muscles in my heart raced.

I had practiced on a particularly warped section of planks in the Pauper Morgue's office. Placing the tip of my boot on the first step, I pressed my weight onto the wood until assured I could plant myself without a crack or noise. Slowly, with a concentrated dexterity unfound in large bodies, I continued this method until I came to a turn in the stairwell. An arm's length more, a turn to the right, and I would be facing the final steps leading up to the bedroom.

Cough!

I nearly jumped out of my skin.

He had to be withered with age, battle wounds, and the heavy weight of the bottle. Moreover, I was no boy and had faced younger, more able men in the alleys of Nilghorde many times over. No matter how much one changes, I suppose, we'll never forget some things, and I came to this realization as I began the first of the last steps. My whole life as a man, I hadn't so much as considered him. Now I was in his home, knife in hand. I made the final climb.

He was asleep under the window. To my right, his dwindled fire still gave off enough light to expose how thoroughly his hair had grayed. The bedroom itself was a mess of chests and bottles. Preparing to wade through, I put away my knife and grabbed what I'd bought from the blacksmith. It was a special occasion, and, after all, I was a poet at heart. I pulled a farrier hammer out from underneath my cloak, then I stepped forward.

Without fail, a board moaned under my boot.

"In the doorway a figure in black, unknown to you, has come to claim you, old man. I have become strong. The menace is upon you. From the crumbling edges of life I have come for you. You taught me to never shut my eyes. You taught me discipline."

When I struck, Father flapped and batted at thin air. Above his eyes, blood escaped, violent and free. His hand gripped wildly for a weapon that wasn't there.

After a long while, after all the twitching had stopped, I opened the window. Like the nameless falling into the Pauper Vault, I dropped him out and refastened its locks. Walking down the stairs, I kept hearing Somyellia: "My beast, look at what you have done." Over and over, finally trailing off with that haunting laugh that could blot out life or breathe it in.

There was one more stop to make, and I needed to get the body prepared. The blanket, now wrapping Father, wasn't the only thing I had packed away. Once my preferred cove was found, I parked the cart and unpacked my cleavers.

In almost complete darkness, I dismantled Father and collected his parts into jars that I'd already labeled.

The scraps were stuffed down a drainage culvert, a feast for the rats I could hear gathering. In less than an hour, I had all the valuables packaged and ready.

Deep into the tiny-eyed hours of night I arrived at one of the reception doors at the Institute of Human Sciences. The groomed gentlemen peering out the viewing port refused to open the door. Holding up a freshly plucked liver, however, turned them around. I had pocketed a few coins this way before, but withered organs and mummified limbs were no longer in demand. Here I had fresh materials. The cart emptied as my purse filled. I called it justified compensation.

By early morning I was back at the Pauper Morgue. After the follow-on tasks were finished, I sprawled out on the floor to finger through the enrollment application the query-eyed doorman had handed me upon request.

At some point I fell asleep. There I dreamed of many things. When I finally woke, all I could recall was a thunderous storm, met with the charge of some unnamable legion.

Soon after, I applied to the Institute. With a successful attempt at their elect entry exam, much to the chagrin of my bosses, I resigned from my position at the morgue.

I signed up for the monastic dormitories and made its space home as best I could. It was strange I was told that I couldn't decorate the walls and shelves with my old tastes, considering where I was, and how it had always served as such esteemed motivation.

The scholarly swarm was quite younger than me, and during orientation I caught the ample look-aways from pubescent faces. Days at the Institute were long and tedious, overflowing with assignments and sapped inkwells far into the night.

Vast does not describe the vaults and exhibits that made the interior. Libraries towered up to ceilings so high their elaborate mosaics were but mere smudges of light and dark when viewed from the ground. There were the fabled viewing cages too. And, if you wanted to venture from the main arteries, you could easily lose yourself in the dungeon-like bleakness, where polished stairs became old wood and peculiar echoes.

The student body rivaled the Institute's vastness so that even I could sometimes get lost in the fray. To my shock, some students were hesitant to handle the muck and piping of our being. That was no issue with my studies, and I enjoyed anatomy class over the more daunting core requirements that left my head a scrambled bowl of confusion.

Dreams are a strange thing. Standing too close to the street performer may often lead one to see the flaws in his act and the streaks in his makeup.

I was passing the courses, though some with great struggle. But I noticed that I never read poetry anymore. My collection of works sat dusty and unused in a corner above all my research papers, scribbled in haste to make punitive deadlines. My muscles ached from inaction, and collapsing into a chair became a ritual after classes. Slowly I began to see my peers as spiritless larvae rather than prestigious scholars.

After a semester, it was clear my life was not in the clean walls of the Institute, or among the kind that never had to fight for their plate. I dropped out shortly after marks were posted. I was tired of feeling sucked dry and hung up in some closet apart from the world. I left numb. Nothing that was shown to me could raise the hairs on my neck or streak wide a smile across my face any longer.

Except for one.

In route from my dorm to my composition class, I would cut through the exhibits. In the Wing of Trauma, displaying hundreds of examples of life's hard edges, I walked past a familiar skull with a hole in its frontal plate.

I returned to the Pauper Morgue, where my return was met with great rejoice. They doubled my old salary, killed my replacement, and with a warm broth escorted me back to my old station, where, aside from a fresh batch of run-through workers who'd proved unsatisfactory to the House of Rogaire, laid many a fair corpse, nude and uninspected.

Such things, so beautiful yet so dead, went to their final resting places uncaressed. The post-mortem with Somyellia would remain unique. Call it loyalty, perhaps.

A Tale From A Good Butler

I: Humble Beginnings

Y NAME IS TYMUIHUS Snier. At least that is the name scribbled on the paperwork at the orphanage where I spent my childhood. I never knew my parents and have honestly given it little thought. A whore and a priest, an actress and a soldier; it all makes little difference to my plight. Having always been on my own, unknowable parents did little but cloud the mind.

The books that I dusted and rearranged had to be worth something. They better—fair compensation for suffering the House of Rogaire, and, in what was a growing likelihood in some peculiar way, the House of Ordrid too.

The books: all that remained was finding an interested and well-funded collector. Verdigris-stained spines could be wiped clean, and with a little buffering, the leather covers could be restored back to their pre-Years of Peace glory.

Although the library was vast, its lack of occupancy was as if its towering double doors were seen by my eyes alone. But the volumes were just the beginning. Treasures hid in unlit rooms and behind cobweb draperies. A stout ladder would able me to chisel out ornate tiles covering the dome ceilings, and just a few of the paintings neglected in the great hall would feed a frugal mouth for years. In a mansion this size, the possibility of finding jewels, heirlooms garnished in guarded drawers, and glorious hidden vaults was worthy of a most thorough reconnaissance.

I hadn't always posed as a butler. I'd been a rent-boy. I'd waded foulness itself having briefly been a grave robber. But, I was always meant to be a burglar. There are essentially two challenges in my current profession. The first: acquisition of a worthwhile target. Worthwhile doesn't always mean the score.

I—

—wait, let me go at this from a slightly different angle.

Everybody squawks on about Do-Gooder's Row—its monstrous white inhabitants and what have you. If you are weary of hearing about them, I assure you your weariness pales in comparison to my own. But perhaps for different reasons. It seems I'm of the select few to take notice, but doers like Zaderyn the Poor Swimmer are in desperate short supply when it comes to finding heroes of the people in this vile city. While the Zaderyns populated the first few columns, the deeds and doers diminish as an admirer heads east, ending at the feet of heroes like the vigilante citizen who reported his overly masturbating neighbor to the nearest Chapwyn temple.

I reckon if you're around a Rehleian long enough you'll hear a peasant's calendar based off when this statue was being carved a necklace or that statue began showing its gauntlets. But perhaps I am no different—a Rehleian after all, and even a Nilghordian, though I admit that last part with the utmost reluctance. So you will have to pardon my provincial ways. It really is the best way moving forward, and, besides, not all of us were born and bred in Pelliul.

With this in mind, during a stint in the Rat's Nest, I shared straw with a couple of thieves. The Do-Gooder statues were all chiseled down to the knees; three-quarters built if you were fortunate enough to study mathematics. We were talking about target acquisition, and those two told me a tale that had with it an unorthodox but long-lasting moral.

At the time, I was rather preoccupied by my draconian arrest. How is it that the more laws made for the greater good, the greater the prisons swell? These two fops—their comical arguing and tragic story captured my interest.

Apparently they'd staked out what they thought was an appraisal loft. Under an assumption that the lavishly garbed old man was the owner, one night they made their entry. Much to their misfortune, the old man was guarded by a colossal dog. To add to their dilemma, the Metropolitan Ward was at the doorstep in a time unseen before by either crook. Naturally, once in the Ward's custody they received a volley of new bumps and bruises. Worst yet, they broke into a loft that wasn't meant to appraise coin and old silverware.

Any committed burglar would suffer a vicious dog to score a worthy prize, but as they took turns being mauled, they noticed no hanging scales or appraisal-loft displays of any kind. The poor fools—out-of-work botanists the moment our land cracked down on a growing list of herbs said to degrade the fiber of the working class—had broken into a bungalow of a Scepter, and the valuables they saw being carried in were gifts to congratulate him on his landslide victory over his mysteriously vanished competitor. In numerous portraits, their would-be victim loomed over them imperiously, or so they described when not choking one another.

Paying attention to the happenings of the city, getting in tune with Nilghorde's heartbeat, led to future successes. Failing to do so led to gallows and grain ships. When I confirmed who the old man was, reality washed over them. That was the reason why the Ward had made it in record time—hell, for all we know, homing pigeons fly to their stations when men of monetary or political importance are in distress.

As I have said, the statues at Do-Gooder's Row back in those days were three-quarters built, which meant the Conqueror's macho quest, over somewhere closer to twenty. Once he'd declared peace in Rehleia, he was, and is, henceforth called The Municipal One.

The Municipal One brought about such wonderful things as new roads, new heroes, and a sea of graves as the goodhearted had a chicken in every pot. With all this came the new laws. Burglary soon came with a life sentence—said to serve as a deterrent, but around the Municipal Dungeon's twelfth or fifteenth grant for another sub-level, the deterrent speeches ceased in the public square. The two who loped into one of the many homes owned by a man such as Scepter Macudden...well, they didn't face a life sentence. They faced what was reserved for unrepentant blasphemers, murderers of the rich, and the rarity: a convicted necromancer.

I try to look for the good in all things. I was eventually released from prison, and in their story learned the valuable lesson of due diligence.

The second challenge of any burglary is dealing with the residents of the target itself. In the case of the Rogaire mansion, I had figured that out like the cleverest street performer. It had been years since I retired from duping spent clients or cleaning out their hotels. I found through careful study that homes were the most lucrative risk to take. The exhilarating joy of standing in an unoccupied dwelling surrounded by the fruits of your soon-to-be labor is mouthwatering. Besides, escalation is the sign of improvement.

I'd been staking out the Rogaire mansion for close to a year. I know you wonder: why wait so long? Why not just get the goods and scamper off? Many would follow your instincts, and there was a time I did as well. That jumpy impatience, however, only results in a minimal score—and, after all, it's the score we all do it for. I shiver at the thought of the money I left in unsearched nooks, mattresses unslit, and rooms behind mirrors. I reckon if I had the patience then that I have now, I would be long retired. Maybe buy a flock of young Suelan boys and live out my days in Pelliul, attending reenactments and theater.

Regardless, I had just about reconnoitered that behemoth place, more a small castle than a mansion. Still, there were locked doors and inconsistencies under floor planks yet to be pried. I had solved almost every riddle, save for the location of a few keys and a peculiar noise I'd regularly hear coming from outside my bedroom window. Besides, despite the high number of reasons that would make any sane person wish to leave, I wasn't leaving until I knew where the vault was, how to get in, and how to gallop off in un-pursued glee.

The denizens of that dreary house were as familiar with my face as they were the gargoyles that stare down from the cornice. It is impossible to repress a smile. Every day getting dressed in the mirror, fixing my bow tie and sash. I am not a big man, lean with shoulders that insist on a mild slouch. My hair, forever blond, now combed over a nagging bald spot. Yet despite such a modest frame and a face referred to as "birdish," I possess the bluest eyes in all Mulgara. Vain? Well, Dear Heart, in two of my careers it was a sad dog that didn't wag its own tail, or know when it could sleep next to the fireplace rather than in a gutter.

❦❦❦

DRESSED FOR DUTY, I tightened white gloves over learned hands and proceeded from my chambers.

❦❦❦

"TYMOTHUS, BRING US THE rabbit," Morlia said, sighing into the hand propping up her chin. Her breath fogged a jewel on her brooch the size of a ripe plum. "The venison has a salty flair."

"Yes, Mum." I went back, past her lounging armored goons, through the steam, and fetched the rabbits from anticipating cooks.

By now our local calendars revolved around the Big Two: Maecidion having been dead a decade—bringing rites and gatherings to the hills and forests and graves that had to be vanquished by our ever-faithful Metropolitan Ward—and the completion of Do-Gooder's Row. Yes, the dearest latter was only a widely rumored two weeks from being finished. I believe the final brilliance to extract from the marble were the bootless toes of some beggar who'd fallen into a puddle right before a Lotgard or Ouvarnian cart had to cake its polished wheels in Nilghordian street mud. As was the standard, the rabbits were in an array of poses, some caught in flight while others in cartoonish gestures of nobility.

For the life of me, I couldn't understand why that family insisted on using trenchers. They had the money to fund the forging of a hundred golden dinner plates without a care. It must have been the late Rinlot's doing, the former master of this ill place. He had been of the southern green hills. An Oxghordian. Those southern voices, with that hilarious booming accent, a continuous melodic blend of aristocracy and farmhand idiot. No matter how long ago a group relocated to the city, they maintained several imperishable southern traditions. He'd been a hunk of a man, the warden of the Municipal Dungeon. As large as a pit fighter, he embraced a regal masculinity in contrast to his rather simple mind.

The lady of the house, Morlia Rogaire—well, I can't recall the maiden name of that redheaded, bejeweled harpy—her family came from the quarter on the shores of the Thunder Bustle and was probably forgotten by her own decree. How those two ever met and married was the grandest of juxtapositions.

He was the one who filled their hidden vaults—wherever those infernal things were. The formidable and overpaid position of Warden didn't explain the wealth. I've seen crazier things in these lands. Although jewels jangled at the bottom of their pockets, they'd never been fully accepted by the Nilghorde elite. The few Ouvarnias who lived in Nilghorde barely acknowledged their existence, and the Lotgards had only invited them to one party.

She, on the other hand, was from the cannibal streets. She still wore her hair tied up for quick bathing and still wore her makeup with the gaudiness of an aging prostitute. A whore, that's my best guess anyway, and it would fit all the better that she sensed an opportunity to capitalize on male dimwittedness.

Once draped in the excesses of wealth, you'd have thought Morlia was an empress from some far-off land. Her knack for barking orders and her eternal dissatisfaction with everything led to miserable dinners and crucified slaves. Rinlot had been a southern boy turned middle-aged man, still hazardously trusting and gregarious. Her eyes carried a keen maliciousness, and her intentions seemed to mimic my own. Yes, she had to have been a prostitute; her cunning business approach to the prize of emerald covered templets and ruby brooches was, in my best mood, admirable.

With Rinlot now dead, the mansion had only three residents. One was Morlia. Another was her and Rinlot's only child, that damned boy Rinmor, or as Morlia insisted for some blasted reason, "Morden." As spoiled as the meat that miraculously always found only the plate of the Lady; his incessant pranks were only dwarfed by his odd behavior. When not trying to trip me with string, I found him staring for hours at the moon.

Last and least, through some intertwining of two family tree's most low-hanging and moss-ridden branches, a cousin of Rinlot's crawled onto their steps years before I took employment and, to my humor, never left.

Werlyle Rogaire-Qell was a humble sight, even for a Qell. I recall from boarding school dreary parchments about their House. Nearly a century had passed since the feud between the House of Qell and the House of Ouvarnia had ended. The regal horse masters of Ouvarnia massacred the House of Qell, sending them scampering to every corner and down every hole in Rehleia. Most now huffed swamp air with the Rehtons down in Amden. A prolific drunk, only his high forehead resembled anything of his much fairer cousin, on the whole short and stubby and always looking down. If he was indicative of the rest, I can at best give them credit for even mustering the gall to challenge anyone in armed conflict.

Werlyle's presence was like an indomitable itch under Morlia's girdle. Since Rinlot was no more, showering Werlyle with insults, often in front of company, had no response other than a few curses and spittle. Half in a bottle of Bleeding Anna on most occasions, his retorts while head down on the dining room table were their own lessons in hilarity. It took every fiber of my being to avoid dropping the tray of exotic slugs when he went into a slurred sonnet. Cobwebs on the chandelier was all the symbolism he required. That and twiddling his nubby finger at her, yelling "loins," and flicking his tongue at the guests who nearly fainted.

"Ah, this should do," Morlia said, as I presented the first batch of posing rabbits. The dinner guests were Morlia's usual entourage, a faceless lot of acquaintances with names I never bothered to remember. "Is there any of that wine left? What was the name of that one? Not that sickly brand from Quinnari; those people truly have no taste for such things."

"Yes, Mum, believe we ha—"

"I remember. That wine we had when—"

She continued her ramble as I thought out the night's rummaging. There was a room in the East Wing whose lock was giving me some real trouble. If the opportunity presented itself, I'd get into her master bedroom. That meant keys. Keys meant vaults. Vaults meant—

Maybe the bitch would pass out from the Grest she was presently going on about. Better yet, one of those sycophants would bed her down in a corner for a few hours.

"Good butler, go find a bottle or two."

"Yes, Mum." I made my way to the wine cellar, chuckling as I heard the predictable foulness from Morlia to Werlyle, whom last I saw devouring his plate at the far end of the table.

When I returned with a bottle of Grest on a silver platter, both worth more than many denizens of Nilghorde made in a year, the fight was in full swing.

"—Leave me alone, you old bat."

"Old bat! That's what you call the woman gracious enough to allow you to stay in her home? You do nothing for us, unless you consider tugging your pecker a chore."

Some of the newer guests smiled through their discomfort, while those who'd grown accustomed to the exchange—perhaps even came to the dinners because of it—laughed loud and chimed in louder.

"No really, *cousin*," she insisted, "what do you do all day?" To her nearest cheering section, "You see what I have to deal with here? Wer-lie-all, such a prole name."

"Same as you, sit on my ass and squander someone else's fortune."

"He really is a boorish type," a man dressed like a poet said.

"You know what Rinlot said about you?" Morlia said.

"Leave me 'lone, bitch. You can entertain these opium heads and cocksuckers with a trip on your broom."

"Is something funny, butler?"

"No, Mum." I snapped to, like a soldier.

"I didn't think so," Morlia said. "I didn't think so because I know you are aware of the stakes in the outer bailey...and their purpose."

That damned Werlyle was going to get me killed. I had to find a reason to excuse myself, and quick. To my good fortune, Werlyle stunned us all.

"I doubt Rinlot had a chance to tell you much of anything," shoveling in his meal, "seein' as you killed him and all."

An air of silence filled the room, palpable and thick. Guest's forks clattered against the table as they excused themselves.

❋❋❋

I SUPPOSE I HAVE gone into a good deal about the others in this particular tale, but perhaps too little about myself. You must excuse me, I am one who looks toward the future voraciously and views the past as burned leaves. Yes, but you are right, sometimes it is necessary to delve into the past. Not to paint the past in gold or fondle one's self with nostalgia, of course not, but rather to make understandable things that are not always apparent—in this case, the alleged interplay between Rinlot and the House of Ordrid, the unalleged interplay between Rinlot and me, and how I came to this wretched mansion.

As I have mentioned, I was an orphan. The orphanage I spent my early years in changed names so many times I've forgotten what to remember it by. Names mean and do little. You may not remember the name of someone or something, but you'll most certainly remember the contents of your interactions. The staff came and went in an ugly merry-go-round of snarls and abuse. A safe haven for just about every form of human depravity, it was also an academy for finding the vulnerable parts of the human body. When not being whipped by the disciplinarians, you had to contend with the older, stronger boys. I learned quickly the frailty of knees when engaged from the right angle, and the sensitivity of eyes when met with a twig.

No birthdays stick out, save one. The fog of early childhood memories unglue themselves. In the spaces between them are swish-swashes of disciplinarians disappearing to fight in the last stages of the wars in Rehleia, and armless and legless veterans hobbling in to replace them. Then came my seventh birthday, clear as summer. The Suelan cooks made me a muffin, shaped like a star with a little yellow candle.

Some of the other boys found it an atrocity they hadn't received a star muffin. After being pinned down, I watched the leader among them, already as big then as your average dockman, stroll up and devour my present.

I got to keep the candle, which I jammed in the eye of the boy who had held down my arm just a moment before. If you push hard enough and hold in place, you can feel a squish followed by a nauseating give. It became a specialty of mine, you could say.

This boy flailed on the ground next to me as the disciplinarians broke through the ring. A man that looked like a shaved carnival ape, known for his heavy-handedness, barreled through, a closing wake of silent children behind him.

I was sent to the cellar, and after his trip to the infirmary the other boy joined me. We were stripped of our clothing and had our hands bound above our heads. For what must have been hours we both just stood there on our toes like pigs at the butcher. He was sobbing into his bandage while I tried to free my hands from the binding leather. With no signs of success, I stopped my squirming as we heard the eminent footsteps echoing down the stairwell. The other boy must have already experienced the cellar. His fidgeting was only outdone by his pitiful squeaks.

I am a man who has never enjoyed coupling with a woman. Mutual exploration of inner folds is exhilarating. But after the whippings and before the march through the bay of eldest boys, I experienced for the first time by sheer agony what would later be an avid joy.

Slavers would come too. They'd pick the stoutest, giving us the added chore of balancing nutrition for self-defense and appearing just sickly enough to avoid being sold to a waiting oar-chain. The same boy who ate my star muffin left us wailing out from the iron bars of a carriage. I gave him a flouting wave, but I'd wager his tears prevented the full fruition of my passive-aggression.

Making it to adulthood and being released was a dim far light. Many ran away. It was my good sense that knew a runaway would just as easily suffer the fates on the streets that they fled from at the orphanage. This kept me there, but nothing else.

Several years later, a well-dressed man roostered in. He swung a cane and was outfitted like he'd just walked off a stage. All of us who were nearing manhood were lined up. He strolled up and down the file until at last coming to me. Clicking his heels when he halted, he inspected me from head to toe.

The boys in the line by that time had forged mighty friendships. It was our turn to exploit the dirt-faced youngsters and run amok throughout. I'll always remember those dearest friends, our savage rise and survival, the secret meetings followed by carnal expedition.

The Lord bought me. Lord Stanifer Voss, was of moderate wealth, but was so embedded in the spectrum of Pelliul exuberance that to many he was as envied as a king.

As he and I made our way in his carriage to Pelliul, I looked back at the frowning monster that had kept me swallowed for so long; I turned my head and uttered an oath.

With polished white woods adorned by golden leaves and seats of red velvet, his carriage was the most beautiful thing I had ever seen. Lord Voss loved my blue eyes. He told me many times. He loved much about me, in fact, and drawing the curtains he showed me the expectations of our arrangement. Although young, I think my developing zest for the endeavor surprised him. Or maybe he already knew.

No, acquiring another lover was not the reason that he had bought me, though it certainly became a perk.

Lord Voss was the quintessential Pelliuli. Arrayed in a dapper style, befitting the more welcoming climate, he would walk into an outhouse as if presenting the commode with an illustrious bequest. Pelliul, known for its festive and extravagant glow lamps, was a buzzing nest of artists, thespians, and narcissists. City of Lights, the lamps hung in every color. The place was not without its Nilghordesque features, of course. A throng of fighting pits, a locust plague of drug users, and the thunderous clamor of the Metropolitan Ward reminded any tourist that it was only part fairyland.

Lord Voss was in the business of entertaining the entertainment. In his gardens, what I would have called fields, he had a healthy stock of opium poppy. Those plants were permitted then as they are permitted now. Their special position in Chapwyn churches passes the law books, but most Scepters owning vast fields of it when The Municipal One and Maecidion penned their arrangements didn't hurt either.

More than the drugs, Lord Voss ran a professional catering service that was at every elite gallery or sold out play. Most auspiciously, he ran a flock of rent boys. That was where I fit in. And the stable of young men, under the grooming eye of Lord Voss, was no inane, filth-laden bevy, mind you. Plucked from orphanages throughout our province, he ran the tightest operation in the city and expelled a hefty sum of money toward our development.

At the orphanage, I was taught the basics in reading and writing. I guess literate slaves are worth more than drooling ones, and the headmaster had to do something with all that time on his hands. Regardless, I am grateful I left there with these tools, because after my purchase I was soon sent to a private boarding school. There I was molded into a makeshift gentleman, versed in etiquette, dancing, literature, and other arenas that had nothing to do with my mindless and naked chore. During my year there, I learned all that I know now about the Rehleian province, its families, loud whispers, and legalities therein.

It was also there where I learned of my greatest passion. Under the oblivious eye of instructors too busy recounting the stacks of tuition, I looted the place of all that could be buried and dug up later.

Upon returning to the Voss estate, I was immediately put to work. As you may imagine, I didn't mind the job. You may or may not be amazed at the different types of clients a rent-boy of value attracts. Politicians, droves of actors, and the occasional insatiable couple would render a chalice of flowing coin.

What a great financial opportunity too. Greed: the mere overindulgence of self-interest. You may call me greedy and I will nod. When I started adding opium to my routine, the floundering orgy turned snoring nudists allowed for the greatest hauls.

I have mentioned the Municipal Dungeon, but theft was not the charge that landed me my first stay.

One morning, I was sunning myself at one of Voss's fountains when he approached me. He advised that I was to be taking a trip. We'd never done this before. The money had to be worth the hassle. Given the address, I was told nothing more than "be flexible." But how many possible meanings could that have in my line of work?

A carnival was wheeling out to Nilghorde that very day. It had been many years, but whatever it was that engulfed me in the back of one of those wagons took me quite a bit of talking to calm myself. Cold swished in my gut when we climbed a small hill, and Nilghorde's jagged fangs shot upward. A haze of smoke hid the summits, and in its grayness I saw what I'd climbed out of. The city smiled a sickness as I confirmed how bad I wanted to turn around. I knew I was *home* when I smelled the sea.

Wanting to accomplish my task without delay, I utilized a bath house and donned my attire. I'd forgotten how aesthetic Nilghorde was not. Back in Pelliul a young man in lavender jingling ornamental flare was as common as the scurrying rodents and cold stares that met me here.

I dodged one heckling clerk, two thugs, three snarling dogs, and a pack of good citizenry nailing fliers before running face-first into the gold-plated chest of a stout Chapwyn priest.

"Those carried by the winds of the flesh," the priest said, "are apteth for collision with more grounded things."

Sitting in the dust and dirt of the street and with my head swirling, I gathered my wits. For one agonizing semester I'd parsed the local religions. Some of the higher shelves in those orders were on Lord Voss's elite list. Of all their screeds and parables, a Chapwyn verse I was particularly fond of, from the same tome this looming clergyman had just spit down on me, had once been inked on a ribbon of parchment I used to unroll in moments of sizzling inspiration: *The rich man needeth not his golden foibles.*

But one I hadn't even realized I'd retained came out of my mouth as the flier-nailers gathered around the priest. "He who useth the Holy Word to mocketh the fallen be both a fool and a brigand."

The crowd spilled from the sides of the holy man and all but flanked me. A calloused hand, though I know not from whom, stopped me from rising. I couldn't help but postulate the sectarian nature of the fliers; some already ripped down the alleys, flapping in the wind. This was the peasantry, the loyal to good order, and some rebel using a priest's divinely inspired words against him was fuel for the burning stakes. A man in rags exposed the first half of a sword.

The priest's ring-laden hand halted the blade. "Offer thoust a tithing," he spoke, leaving a few of his plump fingers on his minion's scabbard. "From thee sinful wages, and be graciously spared thy just steel." The crowd nodded. Some mouthed the words.

Whatever was to come first—negotiations or the unleashing of the mob—was shattered by the Ward. Shooting through the crowd, spinning the priest, and toppling over men and woman alike, a boy emerged from nowhere and ran down the street. The Ward was right after him, a thundering blur of silver and blue, flattening the ragged man and sending his sword chittering over the cobblestones before breaking under pursuing hooves. The filthy youth dropped a loaf of stolen bread and scrambled over the nearest wall.

The gods weave openings in mystery, or so I believed the verse to go. I was on my feet and flying. Soon I was inside the Morgeltine District without a mugging or another near call with dismemberment.

The Morgeltine is the wealthiest district. The Rogaire mansion sits there, although at the farthest eastern sliver and butting up to a dark thicket. A bit of snooping shows the property is considered part of the Morgeltine by jurisdiction alone, and the mansion loomed on the crumbling edge of one of Nilghorde's original boundaries.

The Morgeltine's estates serve as a grand and shimmering moat, one encircling the keep of the Conqueror himself, or The Municipal One if you're the staying-in type. No place in Nilghorde parallels such wealth, and I knew my company for the night was likely to be a man of unquestionable prominence.

I have done so many house calls that I truly forget the mundane trivialities upon meeting at the doorstep. Also, I will spare you and myself from the details leading up to my arrest.

I never had contention with the woman's role; in fact, I made a living out of it. What I didn't predict was literally being ordered to dress up as one. In his bitter drunkenness this land owner, or banker, or Supreme Magistrate spit directives at me like I was one of his slaves. You gain experience, dealing with problem customers, so I tried to calm him and sway the happenings to a more controllable end. He'd have none of it. When I refused to put on the dress for a second time, a showering of threats followed.

Soon the Ward had me in custody. I assumed he pulled one aside and slipped him some gold, fabricated a story to incriminate me, or both. Only when I reached the Municipal Dungeon and was tossed in front of the reception desk did I learn about a new and fabulous Nilghordian ordinance. It was illegal for a prostitute to back out of a "business transaction" after verbal agreement. Since such agreements were impossible to verify, the legal victor was without exception the complainant.

What a vile city! First day back in almost eight years and I'd wound up in jail. Back east I wallowed in décor, mingled with and suckled the rich and famous. Nilghorde, however, seemed my place to be bereft of freedom.

My day in court was a farce. I gazed at the floor as a hot-blooded court room mercenary tore me to pieces on behalf of the absent plaintiff. His screed on the civil duty of merchants would have gotten him booed off a stage in Pelliul, but a stone victory in this urban coast.

For two long years I withered inside the belly of the Municipal Dungeon. I fell back on the learnings of a childhood spent in similar bondage. Steering clear of confrontation as best I could, and strategically inserting myself at opportunities, I made the role of trustee. Being that I could read and write better than most of the guards helped. I landed a position in the head offices—and this is where it all leads—to include the office of Warden Rogaire.

The first time I met him he came storming in while I was busy dusting. "Get the hell out!" was all I heard. Fair haired as I, but with golden brown skin, his hazel eyes made me avert my own as I made a hasty exit. Sweeping, carrying out trash, and taking notes for whomever, I opened my ears as I moused about. I soon learned, among so many trinkets, that Warden Rogaire—Rinlot—had just had a son.

It was like I'd returned to the backrooms of a Pelliul theatre. All the bustle and drama that the guard officers fussed on about was as catty as a group of drunken actresses, just provincial and gruff. One would leave the room to use the privy, and before he could sit down four others who had just sang about brotherly creeds were now gossiping at his expense.

It was in this gossip that I picked up the vital detail: the stinking richness of the Rogaires. Several shift supervisors couldn't get enough of it:

"...A deal with a pirate guild, about the Pelat spice routes."

"No, he goes into Crackpots Range—ever seen those skeletons missing their heads? He sells 'em to the Institute, he does."

"That there boy of his sure squirmed into the life. Probably a team of slaves to wipe then clap after a shat."

They all shared my observations. Rinlot wasn't known for his exuberant salary or his keen intellect. What, did he trip in front of a toadstool-seated fairy eager to grant him wishes? It was said those still dwelled in the wildest glens and dales of the south, but I hardly took it as ostensible.

Upon my release, I bolted back to Pelliul. With some proper grooming, I'd be employable again in no time.

I could have kissed those streets. Cobbled beige and rusted ruby. On Lirelet Avenue the jasmine was in bloom, inhaled as jugglers and fire breathers lanced off the stained glass and gleaming lamp posts.

The portico of Lord Voss's home was as polished as ever. Rapping at the door summoned a housemaid whom I didn't recognize. When I advised that I was a former employee and specified my trade, she gave me the up-and-down then shut the doors in my face. Furious, I beat them until they cracked open once more.

"The master will be with you shortly, sir," the housemaid said through the crease.

After I'd successfully kicked every dead leaf and piece of rubbish off the steps, and as I contemplated another salvo of rapping, the doors cracked once more, then they swung open. Out roostered Lord Voss. I danced on his steps.

He hammered me with the back of his hand. I was cut by a stupendous ring. I stood up only to take note that I'd fell.

"You dare come here now!" He rattled his cane. "I should gut you and donate those cum-bloated entrails of yours to the kitchen of that moldy orphanage where I plucked you from! Do you know what your little stunt cost me? The groveling," he became a parade of *grovelings* and high steps, "the groveling required to keep—the man you cheated—"

"Cheated?!"

"Ohh," dragging out his disdain, "don't you interrupt me. I am in *no* mood." He slapped me again. I fell down again. I curled up in a clump of dead leaves, forgotten by the gardener.

The sight of me crying only encouraged his rage. A furious assault of polished boots and an accurate cane had me soon screaming.

I wish I could have told him. I wish we could have sat down over wine. His grievances could certainly be unlearned, and after hearing my upsetting tale he would have surely shown pity. I wanted to stay in the enchanting light of the glow lamps and frolic among the dainty forever. But wishes only exist in the thoughtful shadows of regret. Reaching down into the dungeons of memory, I went cold and wrapped my hand around a strong twig.

#

AFTER A LONG WHILE I dared to breathe. Voss's eye socket let out its last reserves of blood. I leaned over his flowerbed and vomited out every piece of me that I could.

The air was getting colder. The very leaves that swirled whispered an ill fate if I hesitated. Through my tears, I picked every ornament off of Lord Voss before fleeing into the night.

The doorwoman, the damned housemaid, she was the only one who saw my face. I never told her my name, and I believed no one saw the murder, but I learned fully the one-sidedness of our judicial system.

There were many things on my side. What, were the Inspectors going to chase down every blond man of minor stature to check the grade of blue in his eyes? "Are you a former gay prostitute who killed his pimp? No, be gone then, scum." How laughable. Yet, I couldn't know what Lord Voss may have told his housemaid or what company he'd excused himself from. If the housemaid had even a mediocre memory, a sketch of my likeness was going to be on every lamp post in the city.

I had to leave Pelliul—for a long time, maybe forever.

I was no woodsman and Oxghorde bordered swamp. The former would serve me up as food for wolves, the latter a crippling case of fen-lung. Against every fiber of my being I forced myself to consider my best and only option. There was only one place one could truly melt into the maelstrom. In a week's time I was back in Nilghorde.

Abject poverty alone. Cemeteries with a raven-haired lunatic. And then finally, a mansion to burgle clean.

II: The Noise in the Family Graveyard

SOMETIMES WHEN GIVEN THE opportunity, even the frozen waterfall pours, Ansul's ass, any more trips down Sentimental Alley and I'd be rendered waxing poetically as well-intended, yet arguably as irksome, as Seasmil loved to do on occasion. All I originally meant to convey was I'd learned through sheer happenstance that Rinlot Rogaire was both diffuse and wealthy, the ideal mix for someone hoping to cash in on a final grand theft.

My last visit to the Municipal Dungeon should have cured me of ever worrying about getting arrested again. Not from rehabilitation, no that domain of justice had long flew away by the time Do-Gooder's Row was half built.

There was no rehabilitation in our corrupt city. Prison was now a racket. The class here who hammered nails and baked bread, all hoping to one day also perch themselves in the Morgeltine—well, some had better contacts with the brutes of the Ward than their competitors. Bursting prisons meant fewer merchants to compete against. It meant howling demand for cool-handed carpenters. And good riddance to anyone who made it behind bars.

No, what got me an orientation day flogging and subsequent life sentence was a botched burglary.

I'd started burglaries during the grave-robbing downtime. Our split kept me out of the pauper lines, but Seasmil's strong interests in both the freshly dead and poor made for easy access but meager returns.

The first dozen houses or so were a silken dream. Excelling seemed instantaneous; I was emerging a real natural. Then, on the same night a choir of Chapwyn door-knockers did their civic duty and hung a poet who'd stirred crowds with lamentations of missing our pre-Years of Peace ways, I was caught and my life was over.

Sectarian maintenance of social equilibrium wasn't the only landmark by which I remembered that fateful day. In fact, it became the minor of the two. Upon the fading sting of the last lash, the place was humming. From the dungeon's belly to Rapist Wing, all the way to the shore of Crackpots Range, guards and prisoners alike were bouncing back and forth word that a convicted necromancer was coming in. This was a true rarity. Sorcery, Necromancy, Crystal gawking—the whole arcana bundle that comes with funny children who have more brains than blood—it all had been outlawed in Rehleia not long after The Conqueror and Maecidion the Virulent had struck some deal. The most common rumor was Maecidion's House could still furtively practice all the things Seasmil and Somyellia showed far too much interest in. The only clause was he had to barter new deals with devils. The finer-tuning of which was now lost on the clerk or scribe, but it kept said devilry from stalking the streets and hills, having been as common as cabbage in the far elder days.

Despite the law, a convicted necromancer was something maybe seen once in living memory. The concoction necessary to discover, catch, try, and convict a man who for fun talks to the dead and realigns the very fiber of our natural order was almost impossible. Since the offender often specialized in the manipulation of the malleable human mind, counter-investigations turned to lynch mobs of the inspector and prosecutor. Three cheers. Walls were slopped red, not only in court, but in family rooms of the men misguided enough to spearhead such an uphill task.

Wouldn't you know it, but the giant cage for whipped thieves and cheating prostitutes, or the Rat's Nest, sat directly across the short hallway of solitary cells for "special concerns." I sat at the front as they escorted in a malevolent-looking fellow, barely able to move from all the chains. But no amount of dragging iron did any good. Not long after, he escaped.

✤ ✤ ✤

"NICE BREEZE TONIGHT," WERLYLE said, sounding uncharacteristically sober and approaching from my rear. There was a comfortable wind out. Cool, its currents slipped through the black trees and caressed the balcony.

"Some dinner, aye? Don't know why she insisted on rabbit. Venison was excellent." Werlyle went on. "Those flimsy buzzards that circle her have to be from Pelliul." He sucked on his lip. "Where'd you say you were from again, Snier?"

"I'm from here," I said into my wine glass.

The party long over, I was waiting for the last slaves to retire from the brute chores a butler was thankfully spared—I was more a figurehead, after all, and had my own list of errands.

Werlyle and I talked when the deviations from my reconnaissance and his bottle both aligned. We'd developed a modest friendship, one could say. Mostly to share our disdain for Morlia, I would join him in his chambers for a game of dice or a few shots of a potent beverage.

"What a place," he said, leaning over the balcony as if he'd arrived that day. The outer bailey's wall faded into the floor of the black eastern forest. Squinting one's eyes under a waxing moon like tonight's, you could make out gardens turned wild thickets, neglected statues, and of course the stakes saved for the Lady's wrath.

Girdling the mansion was a wall separating the inner and outer baileys. Equipped with archer towers and weather-beaten merlons, the crenels from above looked to be once defendable, but now were crumbling with the breeze. In the inner bailey, or as Morlia referred to it if she remembered her nomenclature, the lower bailey, were the wells and a stable in front of the grazing ground. No horses lived in the stable anymore, just droves of rodents and the owl feasting on them.

Also in the "lower bailey" was the family graveyard. Staring at me from outside my chamber windows, the graveyard now lay somber below me as the night air weaved in and out of its vaulted obelisks. Werlyle was looking at them as well.

"A Rogaire male has sat in this house since it was built. You know, Snier, that this house is the farthest east in all the Morgeltine?"

"No, I didn't. How interesting."

"Many a marauder and beast used to live in those woods yonder." Tossing a nod toward the black. "Still some lurk in its bosom; it was the first Rogaires to settle in Nilghorde that were tasked with their confrontin'."

As I listened to Werlyle the Defeated carry on about marveled history and a homestead agreement with Nilghorde, my ears picked up a noise. I am in no regards easily spooked—choosing to live in that duplex on Red Wolf confirms that! Wind on the headstones, the rustle of faraway branches, the slave's distant chores: they were the cause of such noise. But scrapes and certain shuffles were not always so easy to dismiss.

"—so after generations, Snier, the Rogaires cleansed all the nightmares emergin'…right off the face of the world."

I paced about, nodding whenever he paused. I found a windblown sycamore writhing next to the base of the balcony, but it made no contact with the wall.

What fiends could have once thrived in the woods a strong arrow shot away? Few nights into my stay, when a full moon cast down from a cloudless sky, I'd seen the skulking and slinking of unaccountable shapes out on the lawns. A cold breeze caressed the balcony, and maybe that was what made me shiver.

"It's a shame. What you think, Snier?"

"Sir, it really isn't my place."

"Nonsense," he snorted, "a butler can answer a question when asked. You're no whipped slave putting away pots. You don't think it's an atrocity the Rogaire ruling this house is an evil-eyed brooch bag? One whose connection here is by name only?" I looked at him for a moment and then back into my long-since-emptied glass. He was of the annihilated house of Qell, and his clinging to the name Rogaire was a desperate and powerful attempt to forget that.

"What of Rinmor? He will come of age soon enough."

Werlyle looked away and bent far over the edge. Scanning from left to right—did he hear noises too?

"Look, Snier, I am going to tell you somethin' you mustn't let get out." He belched into my ear. "Rinlot told me somethin' right before he died, and I honestly believe it led to it. That boy is not going to sit as head of this house. Not fer long. That big-boobed bitch and her melon-headed spawn are going to the bottom of the Black Tongue."

I sat my glass on the ledge.

"Snier, you never got to meet Rinlot. Looks nothing like Rinmor, or should we say *Morden*."

We? And I had surely seen Rinlot, not as much as I would have liked, but that little secret would have to stay with me.

He was right, though; Rinmor looked little like his father. Rinlot had a head like a statue of a Pelat god. Rinmor's was bulbous. The boy's frame was more like my own, and he didn't possess the healthy skin color.

That didn't really cause a big conundrum, though. Children can take after either mother or father; some display features that weren't seen since the days of their great-grandparents. Morlia's desolate beggared family could have worn any and all of the boy's features.

"Why does she call him that?" I asked, figuring if I was forced to talk about them at all I'd at least pull out a question that held some genuine interest.

"I'll get to that, but you should hear this in the order I did.

"Not terribly long before you got here, we had an All Malevolent Masquerade party. The place was crawlin' from top to bottom with fairies, demons, come-back-to-life celebrities. Morlia, get this, dressed up as a peacock." After a laugh, "I forgot what I wore—anyhow, I spent my night at the outdoor bar they'd set up with a pretty young thing, Sammi somethin', all dolled up like a lizard.

"Rinlot spent his night driftin' from one circle to the next. I remember watchin' a Minotaur with wooden horns goin' up and down the stairs all damn night. He had a lot of those men from the dungeon attendin'. Wonder if that lizard came with 'em?"

"What happened?"

"Well, you know the tradition: the boar was brought out to be cut up by the guests in the best and worst costume. You know. But right before it, Rinlot came runnin' outside...to find me. I say, for just a smidge I thought a real Minotaur had bust in the party and was storming my way. He was furious. Barreled my sweet little company right over. Poor darlin' was so beside herself she did some hex before gettin' carried off by a few laughin' guards that were all painted like Suelans.

"He ripped his snout off and embraced me, Snier. I saw tears wellin' in his eyes. When he went looking for Morlia, about feast duties or what have you, Rinlot learned a thing or two."

"Let me guess, she was getting fucked."

"Close, Snier," he snickered, but his intensity hadn't faded. "She was tucked away in a nook with her flimsy buzzards. I can just see peacock feathers and crossdressers gigglin' in some damn corner.

The spiked punch, opium, you name it, I guess it all allowed Rinlot to walk up unnoticed. You know that big statue on the second floor, the crane gulpin' the fish?"

"Yes, dusted it yesterday," I lied.

"He stood behind it and learned his boy isn't *his*."

"What?!" Looking about, I checked my volume. "Come on now, bunch of stoned drunks—"

"Morlia was braggin' about it." Rechecking his own voice. "She said she had met an Ordrid."

And there it was. The House of Ordrid, you've probably heard of them: fully known for their arcane practices, singularity, and madness. Not originally from Rehleia, they were commonly understood as delvers into the blackest of arts. Meeting an Ordrid meant meeting a necromancer, or a witch, and no other name I could think of mustered the same caliber of gossip. They peppered the landscape, their stronghold not far from this very mansion. Since Maecidion's death, however, that stronghold had become more a museum for scholars and macabre teenagers. A few coiled in Pelliul, but word had spread that most now nested deep in the Thunder Bustle.

Somyellia was one, though she had to be dismally low in that House to join me as a flesh peddler. Others were said to dwell in the woods outside Nilghorde and as far as the border that Rehleia shares with the desert wasteland known as Azad. Sailors from Quinnari have told of a city of towers, across the sea and tucked away by a guardian forest. Allegedly, that is where the notorious clan had spewed forth.

But despite all the legends, someone claiming to have merely met an Ordrid was rather common. Hell, I had lived next door to one and robbed graves with her stud.

"Werlyle, are you saying Morlia had an affair with an Ordrid?"

"That's *exactly* what I'm sayin', what *Morlia* was sayin'. Rinlot must've listened for a bit; he told me more. She never said where she met him, but Rinlot and I knew she still had her connections in the Bustle. I still pick out the occasional dinner guest that's prolly a sneak thief. Don't smile; I'm serious."

I knew what to look for, and the only person in the home with a penchant for that work, other than me, was Morlia herself. "Sorry, sir."

"So she meets this fellow and he throws a good fuck in her now and then. Don't know when, but how the hell could I? Poor Rinlot was at the dungeon most days, and he wasn't the assumin' type anyhow. So, she gets pregnant. Of course she tells Rinlot it's his, and of course he believes her."

"Wait, she said all this at a party, tucked in a corner passing around pipes?"

"You don't believe me, aye?"

I was foolish for letting go of my subservient front. His conviction was without doubt; he certainly believed himself. I really cared little one way or the other. I just wanted him to tire out so I could excuse myself.

Shrugs were all I could muster.

He sighed. "I don't know why I am tellin' you all this. Maybe it's just been bottled up fer too long."

"It's all right, sir," regaining my humility, "it's just a lot to take in."

"Well, Snier, I will at least finish it since I started, and you be the judge.

"When Rinmor was born, Rinlot was runnin' all over singin' his praises, right? All the while Morlia was still sneakin' off. But somethin' happened to that Ordrid, 'cause the sly charmer ceased to see Morlia outright. Bitter, she starts to mock Rinlot. I tell you, Snier, there isn't a member at these little get-togethers that don't know what I am tellin' you now. She laughed behind his back and made fun of 'im, swingin' the boy around."

His tone had digressed to growls. Amid the slurred curses I heard something behind me. I leaned over the balcony. The sycamore stared back and I heard a groan, or what had to have been a groan, from the graveyard. Completely deaf to Werlyle's words, I glared, the graves and sarcophagi glared back like the impeccant sycamore. What close-to-death creature had wandered in and now let out these ghasts? I needed to grab a torch, spear, and two slaves to carry them.

A hand placed itself on my shoulder, rendering me a paroxysm of yelps. "Snier, what the devil?"

"Nothing, sir—"

"Enough with the sir shit. I'm no royalty nor do I want to be a part. Again, all this is just kind of comin' out now. Don't mean to put you in an odd way."

My simpering face turned from him and locked back on the nearest graves. "Werlyle, how about we call it a night? Let us continue this sometime soon. I feel there is more "

"There is." He paused, sliding his arm off my shoulder then giving it a squeeze. "There is and we will."

"Please call if you need anything, s—Werlyle." Then he slumped away.

Almost complete silence, save the night noises. Maybe the creature had died? I decided to go down to my room and grab my dagger and a hearty candle.

At my dressers, I realized what was bothering me so. It had been a bit of cosmic irony that I'd given up robbing graveyards just to be assigned quarters next to another one. Outside my windows, the outlines of white headstones and obelisks loomed, distorted by the texture of the glass.

For the longest I'd tried to track down a noise only heard when in my chambers. The sound itself shifted; sometimes a premonition of rats in the walls, the moaning of a crawlspace door yet to be discovered, drunken arm-wrestling goons, fucking slaves, or other times it unsettled my nerves due to its indescribability. But it was one of those things that happened with such regular irregularity that given long enough you tend to just go on without another strained thought tossed its way.

Tonight, however. A sound directly below the balcony meant that it was coming from right outside my window. I didn't wish to will my mind to actually speak it, but there was a chance the noise I'd heard many times was coming from the same place. No logical explanation appeared, the longer I sat on the edge of my bed. With a sturdy fire in the hearth and the dagger tucked under my pillow, I stared at the windows until dreariness took me. Sometime in the night I was awoken by what sounded like a labored grunt, but so faint that I could have imagined it.

❀❀❀

THE NEXT FEW DAYS were a blur. Things were getting too strange to stay much longer. Not least of my concerns, Morlia was not forgiving, and, as much as it pained me to admit, she had an iron memory. A few more insubordinations and I could easily see myself pleading I was no slave as her goons dragged me to the stakes. More than that, I'd located enough loot to rid myself of the servant cover.

The conflict within me howled. The fabled Rogaire treasury was here somewhere. Retirement was out of the question if I settled for leaving without it. Maybe I'd team up with Seasmil again, if I could find him. But an overgrown in dark garb was as common as cabbage in Nilghorde. Besides, a trek back to Red Wolf showed that our old duplex had been leveled and covered in exorcising heraldry. I could keep working. A true professional—and that is what I was—can get out, move on, and let safety conquer hypothetical reward.

But most of all, as much as it nagged me to admit, was that confounded story of Werlyle's. The more time passed, the more his words seeped into my head.

I continued with my daily duties, high-stepping over the boy's string traps, all the while trying earnestly to remain focused on what to take and in what order.

Gold-lined torch-holders were—

Ugh, it was no use.

Regarding the boy, there was the creeping sensation that if I looked at him Werlyle's words would somehow become more and more true. They held at least some minimal plausibility; the impish gaggle, Morlia's taste for ruthless self-centeredness. All of which I could see rooted in a demented reality.

On more than one occasion, I had to pull the boy off a balcony for dinner. The result of breaking the seal betwixt his eyes and the moon was a baying and clawing from the little brat that I hadn't witnessed since the orphanage days. You would have thought he was being carried off to join a grain ship, when all that waited for him were tarts and pastries. Then there was this thing about his two names; what explained such strangeness? And yet looming over it all was the grandest quandary: how did this alleged affair contribute to Rinlot's death?

Rinlot had died when I was in the Municipal Dungeon. Sweeping the floor of a hall nearby, I learned he had succumbed to a gruesome ailment that viciously flung blood out of every hole. The guards who attended his funeral hooted and ranted for days about how awful he looked. Despite the undertaker's best efforts, the corpse put shivers down spines as the lid was sealed.

In fact, it was news of his death in conjunction with knowledge of his wealth that led to my current scheme. What I was shocked to learn, shortly before my harrowing prison escape, was that his widow was refusing to remarry—and, oh, how the brotherhood of guards left their wives to try and convince her otherwise. Popular gossip held that even the Rogaires of higher shelves had traveled from Oxghorde, calling upon Morlia at her doors in their polish and buttons. But she showed them all away. Before long, their outrage decayed to dismay, and finally to sagging departures.

I predicted the droves of suitors lining up to take Rinlot's place. The sight of them, larvae crawling on meat barely dead. What I didn't expect was his widow to show such fortitude. After all, isn't lack of humanity a prerequisite for maintaining wealth?

When I knocked on the mansion doors, my routine was ready. I was but a humble and out-of-work butler, famished from bandits capturing my employer's caravan. Taken to their hideout deep in the woods, I was bound to a tree and whipped for sport. Wouldn't you know my luck, I escaped. All the details were there: how I courageously led the Ward back to the encampment; the old fire pit, septic trench, and even my Lord's girl's dolls strewn about. Alas, it was abandoned. Applauded by the Ward, I was now just seeking humble employment and trying to forget the horrors of my past.

Such a tale would draw sympathy from the recently bereaved Morlia Rogaire, and in case she desired proof, lashes on my back were sure to draw tears. No Lady would question why they looked so old.

A sallow and sunken-cheeked slave answered the doors. After hearing my request to speak to the master of the house, he gave me what I later understood to be a weary look of warning.

After a wait befitting the smuggest of royalty, Morlia appeared. Dripping in jewels and adorned in a ball gown that was unsuccessfully concealing a bust like flour bags, she looked more like a doll than a mourner.

As I commenced with my bit, Morlia stood in complete silence, at some point crossing her arms.

"You have the bluest eyes," she said, interrupting the part where I defied the bandits to do their worst. Before I could continue, a hand was caressing my cheek.

On the way up to her chamber doors, my heart jumped about, not with lustful anticipation but with teeth-like questions burying themselves into me. This was definitely better than having the door shut in my face. Was I to be the next suitor? Did I somehow heal the fickle heart that was leading me up a flight of stairs and into the bed of a man who was still stinking? Was I to be used and then discarded afterward, and did she recognize me from my last profession if that was the case?

What cruel games the fates play. Rinlot had no desire for me, whereas his moll widow wrapped her rawboned legs around me on the first day of our meeting. Wretch. Moll. It is most fortunate I had experience with couples. I shut my eyes and pretended she was Illheador, on stage with muscles glistening as his trademark swagger carried him from scene to scene.

Before I knew it, it was over. As impressed in myself as I was for being able to perform, I don't believe Morlia felt the same. I was indeed given a butler position; apparently the other one had earned a place on the dripping stakes. In the beginning she referred to me as "the new butler that was tortured by pirates, or was it used to live in the woods with escaped slaves," and to my good luck never led me to her bed again.

This all reintroduced a reason to believe that Morlia had been unfaithful to Rinlot with every actor in passing or slave in the house.

But so what? Was it possible she'd fucked an Ordrid, snickered behind Rinlot's back, had the bastard, and was finally found out? Seemed humorously plausible as I put the pieces together. And maybe most jolting of all, though it didn't present as Werlyle said it: I'd spent All Malevolent Masquerade, my favorite holiday, locked away in the dungeon. And Rinlot had died soon after.

Curious, but even dungeons can feel drabber. With Rinlot gone and his foul replacement proving to be even dumber, my wheels began to turn. Soon after, curled up in the bottom of a prison wagon bound for the Institute of Human Sciences, I popped out of a pile of bones and regained my beloved freedom.

When I owned my own mansion, whether in the Morgeltine or elsewhere, I would have to gouge out the eyes of some slaves, and remove the tongues of others. You can't ambush a Pelat, you can't trick a trickster, and you can't steal from Tymothus Snier. Yet, at least in one way, I had been bested.

The fabled Rogaire vault! I'd gladly spend another year in the dungeon just to study this place's layout, learn its deepest secrets, and master its locks. So much would go unplundered, my heart lamented, but my better judgment was telling me that it was time to go.

Werlyle's proclamation that the Moliahenna River would be fed the bodies of Morlia and the boy was rooted in a hateful truth. I had seen the look in Werlyle's eyes, that same black intensity I'd seen worn on men's faces in the dungeon when bent to kill. The last thing I needed was the Ward investigating a missing rich kid. A burglary would be bad enough, a murder worse, but a wealthy person's murder the foulest.

The night's mission came back to me in a burst.

First, go into town; rent the cart and mules. Done so many times at the service of the mansion, no goon or slave would give a second glance at the cart waiting in the inner bailey.

Second, handle the occupants. I had just the thing.

Third, to the library. With finite room, the books would lie on the cart's bed.

Fourth, the mid-weight items and sculptures, followed by the contents of the wine cellar.

Lastly, the fragile paintings, and if I was lucky...everything I could pillage from Morlia's room. I was going back in there; enough time had been wasted, and she would be drooling on some overpriced throw blanket.

My logical hope was that the way to all the stinking piles of gold started somewhere in her chambers. My one unfortunate trip into that maze had suggested one hundred doors could have been waiting behind all the hanging dresses and lip-kissed mirrors.

Werlyle and his contents were to remain untouched. Call me soft, but he'd been a friend in a certain light. Besides, living there seemed cruel enough of a fate.

Then I would be off.

※※※

APOCHXAL: THE FLOWER FERMENTED in my vial. I couldn't remember where they grew, but somewhere far away.

I fiddled with the vial, imagining the side effects as a trapped air bubble responded to my fiddling. This was enough to sedate everyone in the mansion five times over, and the night's order for fetal-tiger soup was most opportune. Slaves and goons would surely finish off what the three would leave untouched.

For insurance, the backup dish was sabotaged with lamp oil. If summoned, the only casualty would be the cook's lives, but sometimes such ruthlessness is required, and every mouth would love soup tonight.

Many would tell you that moments before the actual plunder were like nails being driven past the skull and into the brain. Not me; other than wallowing in the aftermath, the tender moments before execution were my favorite. It was to be savored, looking at riches located, admired, appraised.

Walking past a mermaid statue of jade was like seeing someone whom you had a great appointment with later the same day. Envisioning the process helped steel the nerves: what would go where, how much it would sell for after. I paced myself, calmed myself, and fixed my cummerbund and bow tie to bloom in full radiance.

"Good butler," Morlia said, soft and swift as if speaking to a housecat. "The chandelier needs dusting. I thought I told you."

She was referring to the chandelier in the south hall, not the one here. "Ah, yes, Mum. I tasked a slave to do it. Shall I have him beaten?"

"Well, the responsibility was yours, not some worn-out Serab too busy doing chores that would break the back of a man like you. You can beat yourself if you'd like—later perhaps."

"Yes, Mum," I said, slipping out of the dining hall and heading for the kitchen. That bitch was to see dust and webs on the cursed chandelier for a decade, or better yet two decades.

Emptying four vials into the vat was simple. After warning the culinary staff they'd better start with the backup preparations, they all scurried to the meat closet.

Soon after, the cooks filled three silver bowls full, placing them on a tray that was soon to find a new home. A line of Morlia's ruffians filed in for their share.

"Dinner is served. Baby Hunting Cat soup, with a touch of saffron. Would you be wanting some wine tonight, Mum?"

"No, my head hurts—and don't call it that—and wine with soup is like milk with beef stew."

"Yes, Mum. For you, sir?"

Werlyle looked up. Our eyes locked and it made me flinch.

Walks in the kitchen often met me with glances one would expect from the clump of enslaved men; Suelans, skin glistening shiny black from the steam of the cauldrons. They would occasionally fail to mask their discontent for one of the few free men working. This time, however, they all looked as if found in a bordello by their prudish grandmother, caught gulping the soup by the handful. My best impression of repugnance for their thievery got me down into the wine cellar. The smile afterward hurt my face.

Returning to the hall, Morlia was sucking her spoon. Werlyle stared at the table. He could make a meal into a night-spanning event. He of the Shaking Hand would take up his own spoon shortly. The boy, however, moaned and piddled, swirling the soup with his finger, scowling at me as I passed.

Then I heard it; the thud, clang, and swivel of a dropped bowl.

Maggot of Hell, curse that blasted boy! His bowl thrummed on the floor as he leered over it.

But Morlia was face down in hers.

"Mother?" the boy noticed too. His yellow eyes stared at me as I saved his mother from drowning in her own dinner.

"What the burnin' hell!" Werlyle yelled, startling me and the boy with perfect equality. "Leave her, Snier!"

Uprooting himself, red and bellowing, Werlyle careened through vacant chairs. As Uncle Werlyle approached, blind panic transfixed the boy. His eyes swung from Morlia to me, tender servant standing as I should. Would this be the dinner from Hell, young sir?

"Leave this one to me, Snier!"

I don't think I moved. As Werlyle pointed his finger at the boy, I wondered if his diatribe on the balcony had been some sort of an attempt at an alliance.

"Butler," the boy adjusted, desperately attempting at manners like a shield, "Butler, please stay Uncle."

I saw the ball of webs unraveling now. My best bet was to play it cool and hope that all the goon-guards had enjoyed their soup.

All my fine planning and this was how it turned out. Werlyle had the boy on his knees. Wind from far windows entered the dining hall. I turned away and acted the butler. Milling about the place, "Does anyone need anything? A butcher's knife here, or perhaps a hatchet?" The wind grew in strength, banging shutters at the last beautiful, regal, condescending, vile feast of the Rogaires.

"It's time, Snier! You and me! Told you there was more."
Werlyle growled at my back, the boy pinned down by his boot.
"I don't know how, but that bitch killed him." A furious squeak
came up from below. "Once crossed—stop squirmin'—we resort
back to older justice."

My nerves frayed like gossamer between departing horses. A
descent of thuds and clanks was sure to come gooning into the hall.
But none did. The plan began to reform. Werlyle had spiked the
soup and had attacked the boy. I would cut out his tongue and assist
in dragging him to the dungeon if I had to.

A terrible hiss came up from the floor. "You dare, my father—"

Werlyle reaffirmed his boot to the boy's throat, looking down at
him with eyes that almost glowed.

For the briefest of moments, the squirming corpse in the guise
of a living boy needed my help. A boy was being attacked by a man.
For just a moment, I heard the jingle of orderly keys, but they were
just a whisper in a dream. I found myself replacing Morlia into
her final meal. A gurgle came out as tawdry make-up tainted the
broth. I told myself it saved her from a more gruesome end. Perhaps
I was right.

I walked out, not as a man ready to begin a mighty pillage, but
sulking and unwound. The yelps and drunken curses behind me
were penetrated by snores of sedated guardsmen.

What now? Kill Werlyle? If I didn't, he surely lacked the cunning
to cover up a double murder. The dungeon, I knew all too well,
had many innovative techniques (and overzealous technicians) that
would easily get my name out of his toothless and spurting mouth.
If I killed him, it would have to be by force, which would leave a
wound. To the gods I wished Seasmil were here. Maybe I could
get lucky, stab Werlyle in the gut, and make it look like a maniacal
murder-suicide.

Why did the fool have to pick tonight to initiate this sloppy act of violence? What I guessed was a voice box getting crushed made a rubbery sound as my face sunk into my hands.

Wind howled through the windows. A good butler would have shut them. I began to rise.

III: Quarrel in the House of Thieves

WELL, WHAT WE DO now, Snier, bury 'em?" Werlyle said, staring up at me.

Great—I was involved with murders in two provincial cities. I had returned to Nilghorde out of necessity. Now that I was quite capable of being put to death in both, was Pelliul the new old destination? I certainly wouldn't be the only criminal bouncing from one giant to the other. But my pragmatism won: Oxghorde and its addled silly midget of a neighbor, Amden, would have to do, fen-lung syndrome and all. But only if I figured out how to deal with Werlyle.

"The goons won't sleep forever," I sighed. "We are in this together now, whatever *this* is."

"That we are, Snier, that we are," Werlyle said, slugging to his feet over Rinmor. Werlyle wore the boy's struggle in the form of glistening scratches.

A furtive hand reassured my dagger was still tucked under my sash. If he demanded to sit on the mystic throne of the Nilghorde House of Rogaire, a confrontation was inevitable. He would deem the mansion, and all property therein, escheated to him. He likely thought I just hated Morlia, and it was enough that her body cooled with the soup that claimed her.

"Snier," my name lingered—not furtive enough—"what are you up to?"

"The servant role is over, old friend. Afraid we're about to have a bit of a disagreement."

"Don't know what you did to that soup, but I'm impressed. Bitch deserved worse. I wouldn't have thought of that. Remember, though, *boy-o*, I'm not goin' to drown in some broth for you."

He stepped over the boy.

We must have looked like some pathetic interlude, ready to do our act for boos and drunken revelry before the main event in a fighting pit. The butler with a limp wrist and a dwarfed drunkard, battling with all his might to avoid swaying. At his next step forward, I drew my blade.

Werlyle turned and looked at Morlia. He walked not toward me, but to her. Sweat from my palm ran down my dagger as I watched him cradle one of her hands. A fight began to look less likely and a necrophobic bout of petting more probable. He slipped one of her rings off her finger.

"You know what this is, Snier? The matriarch ring of this House. A Rogaire Lady has worn it as long as this home has stood on the earth."

I flinched when he tossed me the ring. But I caught it too.

"Now," he said, pulling up his soggy trousers. "Times drainin'. Let's bleed this place of anythin' these miserable ghosts would care to haunt. Aye?"

"How long have you known?" I gaped. Watching his chuckles and ticks, his odd signature of laughter, I realized there were two snakes in this nest, and their tails were interwoven.

"I was working somethin' similar, drinkin' water out of a Bleeding Anna bottle most days. Long before you got here I came fer my own reasons. Rinlot up and died on me though, and that got me thinkin' a bit scandalous. I got to say, you really showed me a thing or two on patience. You're a planner, aye? I'll tell you what I am, Snier: a survivor. Figured you'd pull off whatever upstart you had cookin' before too long."

"But?"

He undulated like it stung, or tickled. "I saw you slitherin' about the place. 'Sides...you talk in your sleep."

###

JOINING FORCES TOOK LITTLE explaining, and perhaps I shouldn't have been surprised. Werlyle even added to the exploitation with a simple detail, so in front of my nose I almost smacked myself for not thinking of it on my own.

"I bet she has keys on her, Snier." My mind began to recalibrate. "We may not have enough time to get everythin'. What'd you put in the food? How long's it last?"

"That is absolutely no concern," I said. "Everyone in the house sucked it down and will be waking up this time tomorrow."

"Can't be too sure, though, aye? You think we need to take... further measures?" His eyes widened.

"Not necessary."

"But we can't be too sure, right? We don't want some thick-necked guard, happenin' to have a hearty constitution, chasin' us down or runnin' off to the Ward."

Rinmor turned out to be but a precursor. Werlyle ran as a man does when rotted by the bottle and owning stubby legs, around a corner and up the stairs. Finding the first of several sleeping goons, he relieved one of his sword and then dashed about slaughtering the lot.

Astonishment fails to grasp the feeling of watching the drunkard skewer a score of guards and slaves; not a ruthless swordsman, but more a pudgy child on a bright outing. The irksome noises of hacks and grunts, met with an occasional moan, echoed about the place as

I did my best at staying focused. As he darted in and out of my sight, messier each time, I made my way to Morlia.

Her slumped state made my actions no less nauseous. Nothing was around her neck but a necklace lined with star sapphire. Removed and put in my pocket, I patted her all over, desperately wanting to feel something solid. After running my hands inside her girdle, I fingered through her wetted undergarments. Between her thighs, nestled snuggly against her pelvis, the ring I'd put on my finger came on a sudden *ting*. My fingers clasped around them. From that unholy perfumed trench I pulled out the keys. Two, one large and one small, dangled on a golden ring.

Dark, thick ribbons of blood trailed off Werlyle's arms as he reentered the dining hall. Panting, he was still taking excessive and bizarre routes in his search for additional victims. His gut protruded from his ever upward-crawling shirt as he exerted himself to a blissful exhaustion. The keys had found my pocket in a flash, but as I planned on explaining that no such keys existed, he exited to enter a dark nook where apparently someone still lived.

My excitement was incapable of restraint. What vaults those walls would surely contain. What we would pack into the cart together would be impressive, lucrative—quite, in fact—but it wasn't statues and paintings that had lured me.

"Snier," Werlyle said, emerging from the nook and brandishing his dripping sword. His boots emitted a mushy sound as he left a remarkable path of footprints. "Okay, think that's all of 'em." Restarting his ticks, "One cook wasn't fully out, drunk on whatever you did, and those big white eyes were so pink and hazy. He thought I was some ghost or god those spearmen worship. You seen those little wooden idols they have up in the kitchen?"

Werlyle had surely earned my attention. The toad, in plum and blood, fooled the eye. He was a plug of some visceral tissue that oozed out of a wound or woman's loins. But he also killed. As much as I had confidently calibrated him, and at some moments even pitied him, he had transformed before me into a man that was to be treated as a genuine maniac.

"Yeah," he continued, "I think he thought I was one of those. How he prayed—"

"Let us get to work," I said, hopefully appearing unmoved.

"All right, all right. No rush as I see it, but I'm not the mastermind here. What shall we do now, sir?" He bowed low, like a butler.

Two hefty table covers later, we were in the library. All six volumes of *Poems of the Classics*, the legendary Denom Vandahl's *Transient State of Grace* and *Songs in Regal Twilight*, *The Embryonic Sorcerer* and many more I pulled from their shelves and dropped in Werlyle's blood-covered hands.

The sight of them made me have to consider: Was this come-to-fruition maniac done with his bloodlust? Was he even capable of splitting the loot and then merrily go about his affairs? Was I, Tymothus Snier, willing to do such splitting?

I knew from too much time in the dungeon who'd squeal. If he got caught—and with an array of bloody boot prints and his reckless blabber-mouthing, he would—it would only be a matter of time before I was in some pre-disembowelment pillory. Equally troubling, he was possibly brewing a similar plan, trying to make my grizzly death look like a grand murder-suicide, swaying in his retelling to the Ward.

"How fuckin' heavy can a few books be?" Werlyle grunted as he toted an improvised satchel across his shoulder.

"You'll be surprised how much some of these will sell for. Besides, they're not that heavy." Hugging my much smaller load, it was relieving to pretend I wasn't bothered. In time, my temperament began to follow suit.

I freed one hand long enough to open the door that led us out to the bailey. From over my stack of books, I saw the pale tops of the obelisks. The wind wasn't just strong, it was cold. I walked to the cart, Werlyle in trace. After placing one table cover at its base, Werlyle handed me the books and I made a solid bed of literature. I covered the second linen over them and hopped out.

Next were the sculptures, silverware, candleholders, decorative weaponry, vases, curtains, sconces, and a plethora of odds and ends, all packed into their waiting crates that I'd kept cached in the mansion's heap of undisposed garbage. Thieves in the night; Werlyle bellowed in mirth, impressed by my puzzle-piece packing. I stood atop the boxes, cold wind blowing my hair wild.

"Attaboy, Snier," Werlyle laughed. "Oh, did you check Morlia? Watch it. Careful, Snier, don't go droppin' boxes and lookin' all amateur on me."

But I didn't hear him. My heart pounded, my comfort annihilated, and I knew it wouldn't return. "She has to have keys on 'er." Werlyle said. "We find what we're both really lookin' fer—hey, how we goin' to fit it all? Make another trip?"

After a moment: "No, one trip is all we can afford, and no, I haven't checked."

Rinmor lay dead on his back, eyes wide as his mouth. Werlyle tossed Morlia about like a sailor emptying his duffle. The gown ripped, her red hair an unkempt mess dripping cold soup, her face placid, like a doll's. When he lifted her upside down, her head hit the floor stones. The sharp, crisp smack made my belly turn.

"Arhh," Werlyle roared, "they got to be here!"

"You're right," flapping in exasperation, "there's no other place they could be. Wait—some hiding place outside her door?" That corridor was so thin only one of us could check the tile or trim at a time, and I knew who should lead the file.

"Fuck!" Werlyle dropped Morlia like she had bit him. "I didn't come for books."

"Me either, friend. Let us at least concentrate on said books and decorations for the time being. Maybe our minds will re-stir. I have often found that—"

"What's next?"

Small crates of wine, along with dozens of Black Monk, Spiritual Oppressor, and Bleeding Anna fit snuggly in the wagon that was starting to creak from the weight.

A hellish moan came up from somewhere behind us.

Werlyle screamed and flapped, pelting me with congealed blood and dropping a crate of Grest.

"I don't know," I said to Werlyle as if he'd asked me what made such an awful noise. And I didn't know, not completely. But I wasn't in complete denial either. The final result of my grim induction was that something stirred, and had stirred a long time, amid the tombstones. There wasn't even the luxury for conjecture; this time the noise continued.

Many may condescend from their comfortable parlors the actions we then took. No bother, there is no way to make rational what was occurring, nor make rational our response. Without a word, we walked side by side. We walked toward the noise. I unsheathed my dagger as Werlyle wiggled the bloody sword out from his belt. I knew the source far faster than my mind would officially admit. Our walk toward what was now a series of grunts and thuds ended at the foot of Rinlot's sarcophagus.

The wind had picked up to a near approaching storm. Thunder rolled in the distance. Lightning lit up the west. Maybe the weather was trying to mask our discovery. For the faintest of moments, I thought I saw a pale face between two obelisks, but before my eyes could strain further, Werlyle pulled me away.

"Snier, this is Ordrid work."

"Maybe, maybe—but maybe some animal burrowed in from the bottom," I said, trying to believe it.

"I have to open it."

"What!? Whatever's in there is better left *in there*. Remember why we're here. Grave robbing is *not* an interest, or important." My free hand clasped the keys in my pocket.

Werlyle placed his ear to the stone. "It ain't about robbin' it. They have a curse on him, don't you hear him," rolling his gaze up to my own, "in there?"

No! I didn't! I heard some terrible moan, but it didn't have to be from where we stood. It was an awakened guard, not properly run through, clamoring out into the night while regaining his wits. I tried to convince Werlyle of this, but it was no use. Thuds burst up from within, and when they did even I finally conceded the most terrible of realities.

Sentiment comes at the oddest times, and certainly nothing odder than the moment before us. Despite all my current dilemmas, I began to wonder if maybe some form of white magic was available to help the thing that now pounded up against the inner stone. For a king's treasury the Chapwyn priests would maybe put down their incense-swingers and emasculation tools to evoke some assistance. I listened for words, something to discern that the pounder was in the realms relatable to the human experience. I strained, but nothing.

"Snier, I'm opening it."

"Wait—"

Of all my knee-jerk reactions that have surprised, I found myself pushing Werlyle aside to slide the lid myself. As my dagger's blade and fingers felt the stone separating, I held an image of Rinlot's somehow golden-brown skin next to mine, how grateful it was to be saved, and how forever in my debt it would pleasantly remain.

The stone was heavy, and I eased off to regain my strength. Taking in a breath, I looked up at the night sky. The gargoyles atop the corbels loomed down as they always did. Maybe it was just the darkness, the whirling of the leaves, or my severely jostled nerves, but they all seemed different. More *perched* rather than *placed*, as if waiting for some command unknowable to us to take flight. A little one I'd never noticed before, looking more like an imp from a bad fairytale, seemed to have eyes that moved.

The lid gave with a sucking sound. Through a sliver of blackness, fingers stretched out and into the open air.

Werlyle flailed back, shrieking and cursing. I possessed neither the ability nor the inclination to look back at him. The skin was brown, but to a leather. Fingers, their tips worn to the bone, appeared to be searching for something.

I had expected this abomination to toss the stone lid next, send it down in pieces, and emerge to wreak whatever havoc its unfathomable torment would see fit. Instead, the fingers vanished back into the sarcophagus. Without the pure stone to muffle them, all that emitted were sobs and moans of the lowest despair. There was rage possibly, but a rage of the rat in the trap, back broken.

The terror possessing me froze my ability to run. Aghast—the thought of me sleeping, while out the window tossed and turned this afflicted carcass. He—it—felt pain, or at least perceivably so from the noises he made. Rinlot, or whatever he was now, was unable to emerge from a confinement that even I was able to pry. Pity blocked my throat when I contemplated if an intelligence, some residue from his time among the living, lingered, him knowing full well what treachery put him there. Whatever emotion I may have felt next was destroyed as lightning struck the bailey.

⹋ ⹋ ⹋

WHEN I AWOKE, THE world swayed and pulsated as I found myself getting back on my feet. A pat-down gave me reason to believe the lightning hadn't struck me. With a wobble, I regained my senses.

I couldn't have been out long. The wagon was tearing out of the bailey, heading for wherever a pair of scared mules would decide.

That hideous hand had once more emerged from the open space, this time grabbing at thin air. My run for the wagon only sent me back to the ground. Rolling from my stomach and clutching my shin, I turned to see that the crate Werlyle dropped had bested me. Rain peppered my face as I stood once more.

My eyes then held the greatest of their disbeliefs.

Werlyle was on his knees, clutching his throat with both hands. His vocal tubing gave a rubbery squeak as the thin blade of a rapier returned to its scabbard. As Werlyle hit the ground, the boy stood over him.

In the open door, atop the small flight of its steps, stood Morlia and someone else. This second person, a man, I could have sworn I had known.

Maybe it was the moonlight, the lightning strike, or my blood rushing away from me, but her face, as the boy's, was not the same. Some form of unlife had replaced them, and its new demeanor I dared not guess. Their features were somehow more canine, their eyes beady.

Standing like figures claiming the summit of a nightmare wedding cake, I then knew with absolute certainty who the other person was.

"Morden," spoke the Ordrid. The boy ascended the stairs, coming to his father's side. Morden turned toward the graves. A pang of sheer terror erupted once more when they cast their eyes on me.

You'd think I would have run, but I didn't—couldn't. I stood as lifeless as a statue in that long-gone mule cart.

❈ ❈ ❈

THE NECROMANCER'S DISAPPEARANCE FROM the dungeon surprised no one. Those with a penchant for gambling placed bets on the manner in which he would bust loose, while those prone to superstition debated what manner of ghost or beast would be summoned to assist in his freeing. All were wrong, and it was the nonchalant reaction of Warden Rogaire that now made sense.

Soon after the necromancer was paraded, in that most ridiculous presentation of chains, I was fulfilling some trustee role on the outskirts of the head office when the warden had him brought in. They remained in his office long past when I was returned. I always assumed some long-winded interrogation had taken place.

The Ordrid's escape happened to follow that fateful meeting. In conjunction with a curious guard change that night, Warden Rogaire had his lower tiersmen come join in one of the dungeon's most famed spectator sports.

Prisoners who'd failed on debts to royal houses, or who particularly irritated the guards, would be tied to a stone altar. Naked as the day they were born, a guardsman would soak the backside of the flailing prisoner with bitch urine and then release a pack of deprived Imperial Hounds. The fight to get to the scent was as brutal as the unsettling result. The honor to attend was normally reserved for only the ranking cadre and occasional whores that occupied the key-vaults in the not so quiet hours of roll call and gruel distribution.

Rinlot couldn't have known that the sorcerer, or necromancer, or whatever title best fit the man who came to him in chains before leaving at leisure, and who he foolishly bartered some deal with, was the very man who sired Morden.

Was imprisonment itself a part of the Ordrid's plan?

###

THE ORDRID LOOKED AT me, or through me. I felt as if I would fall and never stand again.

Not through my own mind did I see what I say to you now, but through where my eyes may have been if I had been in league with the Ordrid and standing, fittingly, a bit to his rear:

I knew the place all too well. The gate of the Municipal Dungeon was built as if for giants. In front of its iron scales, each alone as large as a shield, two guards leaned on their halberds. Standing in front of them, the Ordrid was clad in black leggings and a dark coat. Its hood hung behind him, tapering down to a point near a thin waist. His head was bald like an onion. His hands moved along with his plea, reassuring and coy.

The bewildered guards couldn't decide who to gape at longer, one another or this man, in the midst of a full confession stating he practiced all the outlawed magic. Some time must have passed between that image and the next, but the Ordrid—surely this fiend who rose Morlia and Morden—the Ordrid then turned to *me*.

He had wanted at Rinlot even more than I. For reasons I would never know, now he would have Rinlot's family, his wealth, and toast fine glasses to having caused such misery. The next thing I saw was he and Rinlot walking out of the front gate. Night had fallen. The two walked like friends. I saw Rinlot's eyes, in some fashion glazed over beyond their usual simplicity, and then I see it. They shake hands. My mind's eye, or whoever's, locks in on these hands and does not move after.

###

WIND WAS IN THE trees and rain pelted the gravestones. The three of them descended the stairs. I stayed like a cornered hare.

"Morlia. Sir, a great tragedy has befallen this house tonight. Your cousin, as you have readily identified as the perpetrator, has poisoned your slaves, your guards, and I thought you both as well. I caught him here beginning to loot our dear Rinlot's final resting place." I pushed out a grin, or it felt like one.

"Sir, I beg of you—" They had neared to an arm's distance, walking solemn and in unison. Morlia's eyes were two black stones above lips whose opening could have contained rows of fangs.

A hand grabbed my ankle, another my belt, ripping it off of me with tatters of my breeches coming with it. Breaking free of this terrible freeze at last, I felt for my dagger, but it must have lain somewhere amid the fallen leaves.

Stone slid with wet grittiness. I found myself looking up at the leering gargoyles. One of my hands pushed against Morlia's face, which appeared in an instant far less dead. My other hand was clasped around her keys in my pocket, and then they too were taken from me.

Epilogue

TYMOTHUS KICKED AND SCREAMED, bit and pled. Morlia slid open the lid as Morden and Irion stuffed him into the sarcophagus. The once summer-hued skin of Rinlot, turned coarse and loathsome, clung to the new inhabitant.

As the lid slid back, Irion Ordrid's grin grew as wide as his son's. Sons were a theme. It make have taken too many years and two bodies, but the Ordrid soul who Rinmauld had cheated finally avenged the Ordrid House, and sent Rinmauld's into tortured ashes, his dearest son moaning in this delightful little box.

Rinlot's hands found holds on Tymothus. Just before the lid was sealed, and what was left of the light of the moon would be conquered by forever black, Tymothus dared look beside him. Rinlot stared back, the agony of hell on his wry grimace.

Leaving a wake of bursting bottles, the runaway mules careened out of the Morgeltine. The last to see it in the district was a bloated Wardsman, watching in disbelief as a ghost-driven wagon wheeled past.

The beings that haunt the dark weren't limited to the Rogaire Mansion that night. As the wagon entered the celebrated Do-Gooder's Row, flowers and confetti and strands of human hair were kicked up by its wheels. The mules' hearts finally exhausted, the shadows stalking the nooks and miasma of Nilghorde began to envelope the cart.

Some would suggest more Ordrid magic was at work, but the mob was just the poor, the slowest five among them sent to the Pauper Morgue.